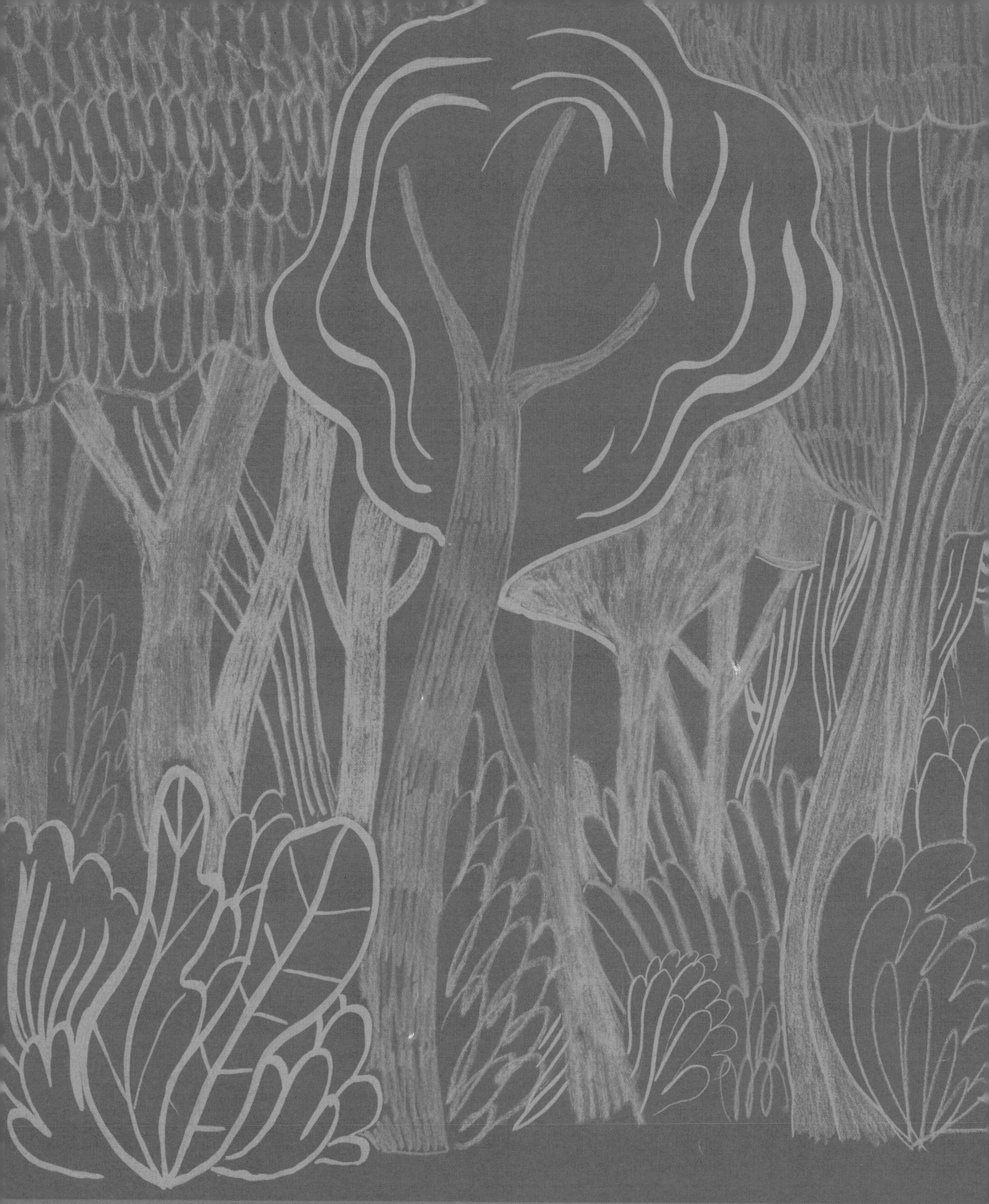

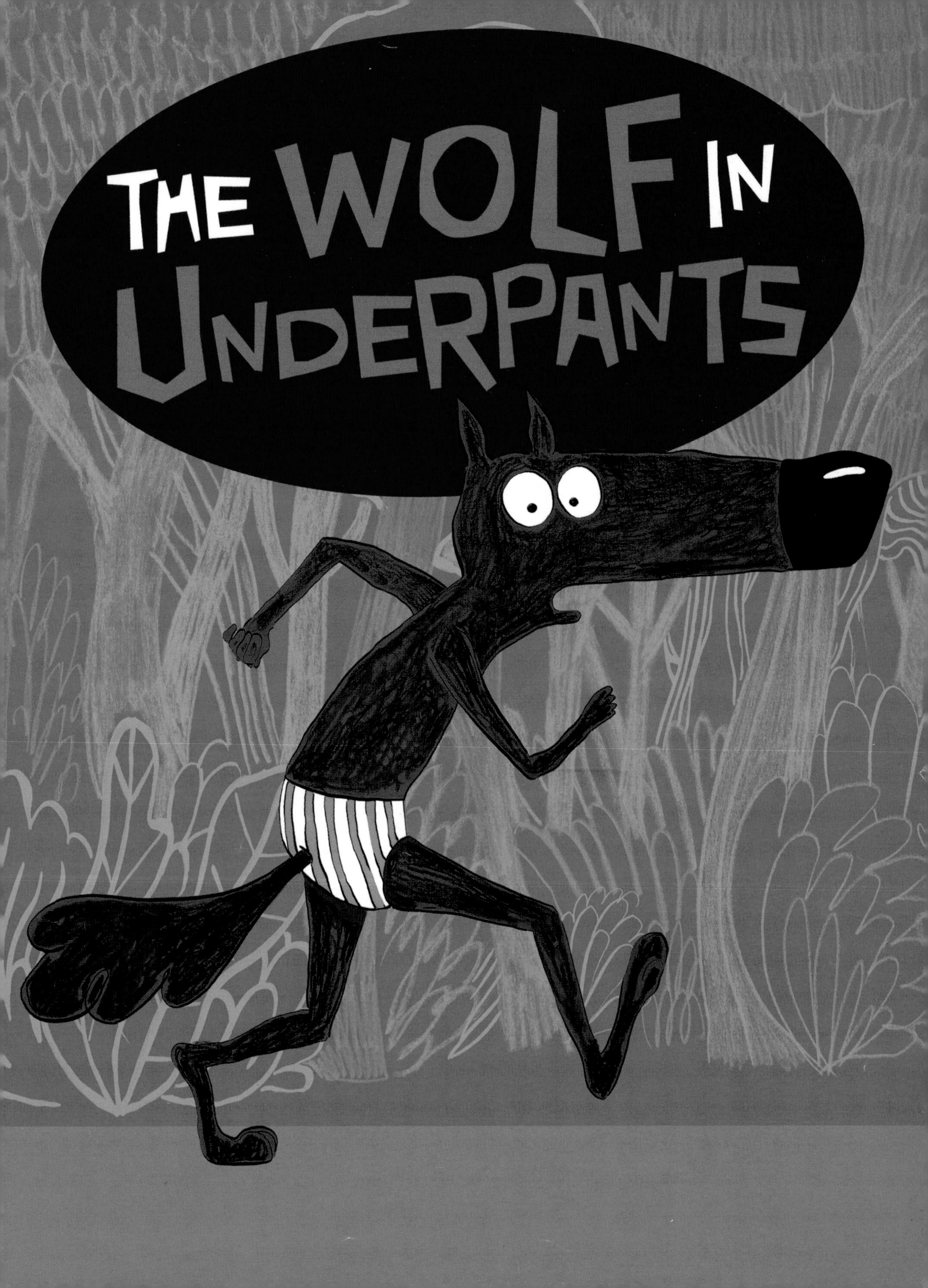
THE WOLF IN UNDERPANTS

Story by Wilfrid Lupano
Art by Mayana Itoïz
With the friendly artistic participation of Paul Cauuet
Translation by Nathan Sacks

First American edition published in 2019 by Graphic Universe™
Published by arrangement with Mediatoon Licensing - France
Le Loup en Slip
© Dargaud Benelux (Dargaud-Lombard S.A.) 2016—Lupano, Itoïz, and Cauuet. All rights
reserved. Original artistic director: Philippe Ravon.
www.dargaud.com

English translation copyright © 2019 by Lerner Publishing Group, Inc.

Graphic Universe™ is a trademark of Lerner Publishing Group, Inc.

Graphic Universe™
A division of Lerner Publishing Group, Inc.
241 First Avenue North
Minneapolis, MN 55401 USA

For reading levels and more information, look up this title at www.lernerbooks.com.

Main body text set in Stick-A-Round 13/15. Typeface provided by Pintassilgoprints.

Library of Congress Cataloging-in-Publication Data

Names: Lupano, Wilfrid, 1971- author. | Itoïz, Mayana, 1978- illustrator. | Cauuet, Paul,
    1980- illustrator. | Sacks, Nathan, translator.
Title: The wolf in underpants / Wilfrid Lupano, Mayana Itoïz, Paul Cauuet.
Other titles: Le Loup en slip
Description: First American edition. | Minneapolis : Graphic Universe, 2019. | "Translation by
    Nathan Sacks"—Title page verso. | Summary: After living in fear of the wolf with crazy
    eyes and fangs like ice picks, a forest community is stunned when he shows up looking
    calm and wearing striped underpants, leaving them wondering why they were so afraid
    of him.
Identifiers: LCCN 2018014450 (print) | LCCN 2018021439 (ebook) | ISBN 9781541542730
    (eb pdf) | ISBN 9781541528185 (lb : alk. paper) | ISBN 9781541545304 (pb : alk. paper)
Subjects: LCSH: Graphic novels. | CYAC: Graphic novels. | Wolves—Fiction. | Forest animals—
    Fiction. | Fear—Fiction.
Classification: LCC PZ7.7.L86 (ebook) | LCC PZ7.7.L86 Wo 2019 (print) | DDC 741.5/973—dc23

LC record available at https://lccn.loc.gov/2018014450

Manufactured in the United States of America
1-44701-35532-6/8/2018

THE WOLF IN UNDERPANTS

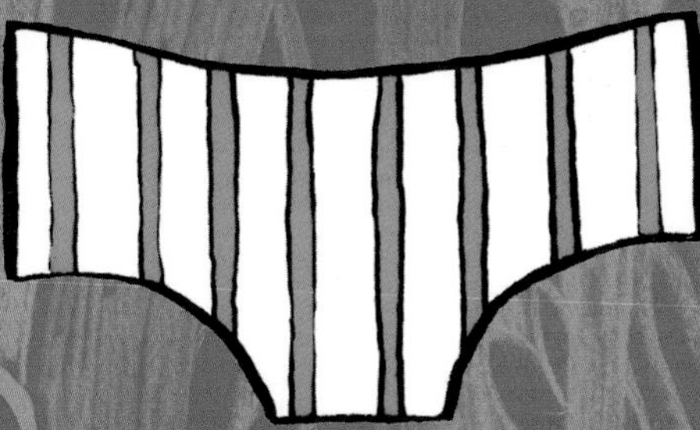

Wilfrid Lupano

Mayana Itoïz
and
Paul Cauuet

Graphic Universe™ • Minneapolis

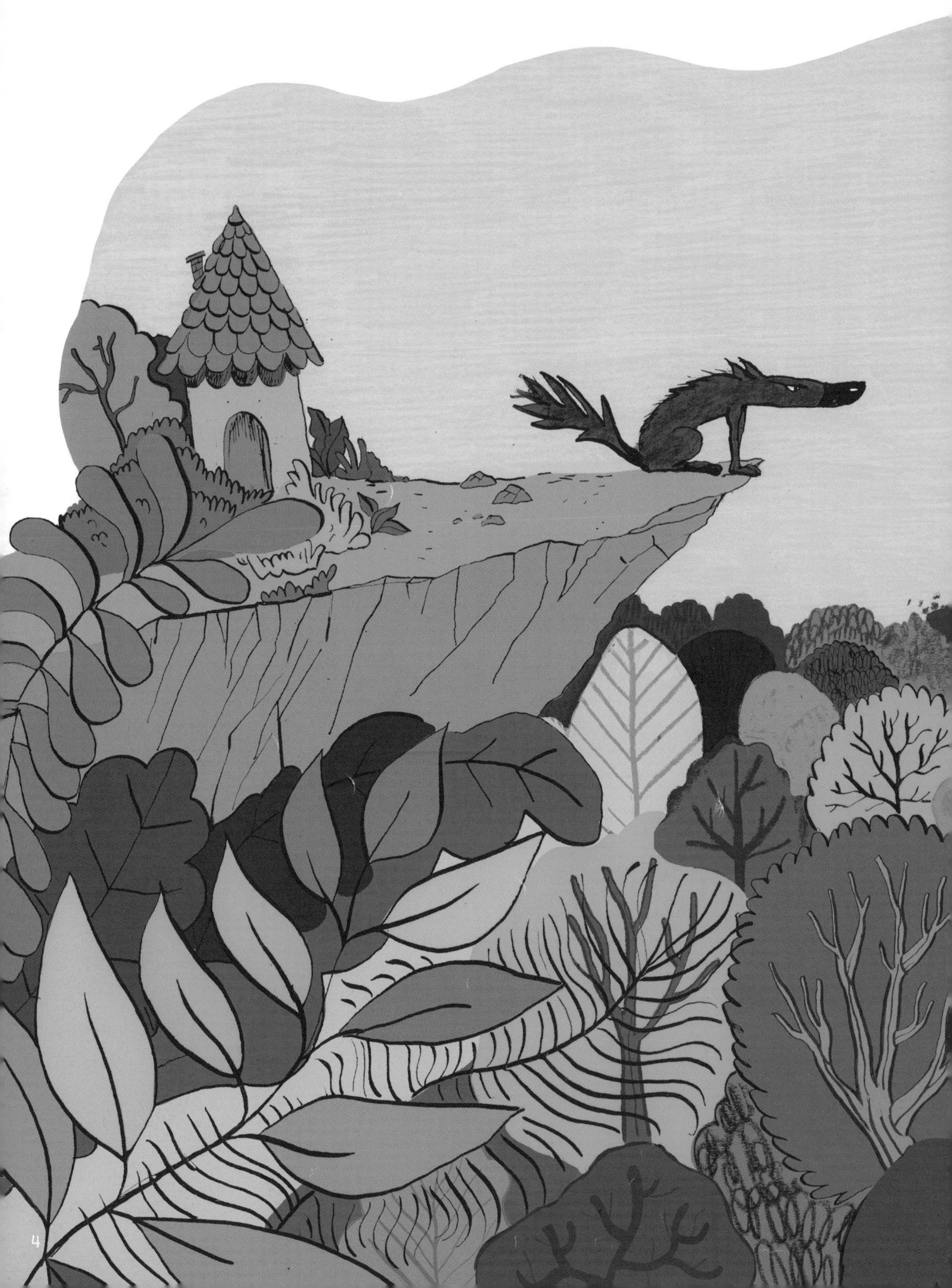

HIGH ABOVE THE FOREST LIVES THE WOLF. AN ICY CRY. CRAZY EYES.

IN THESE WOODS, WE KNOW TO MOVE OUR BUTTS WHEN THE WOLF COMES DOWN TO EAT.

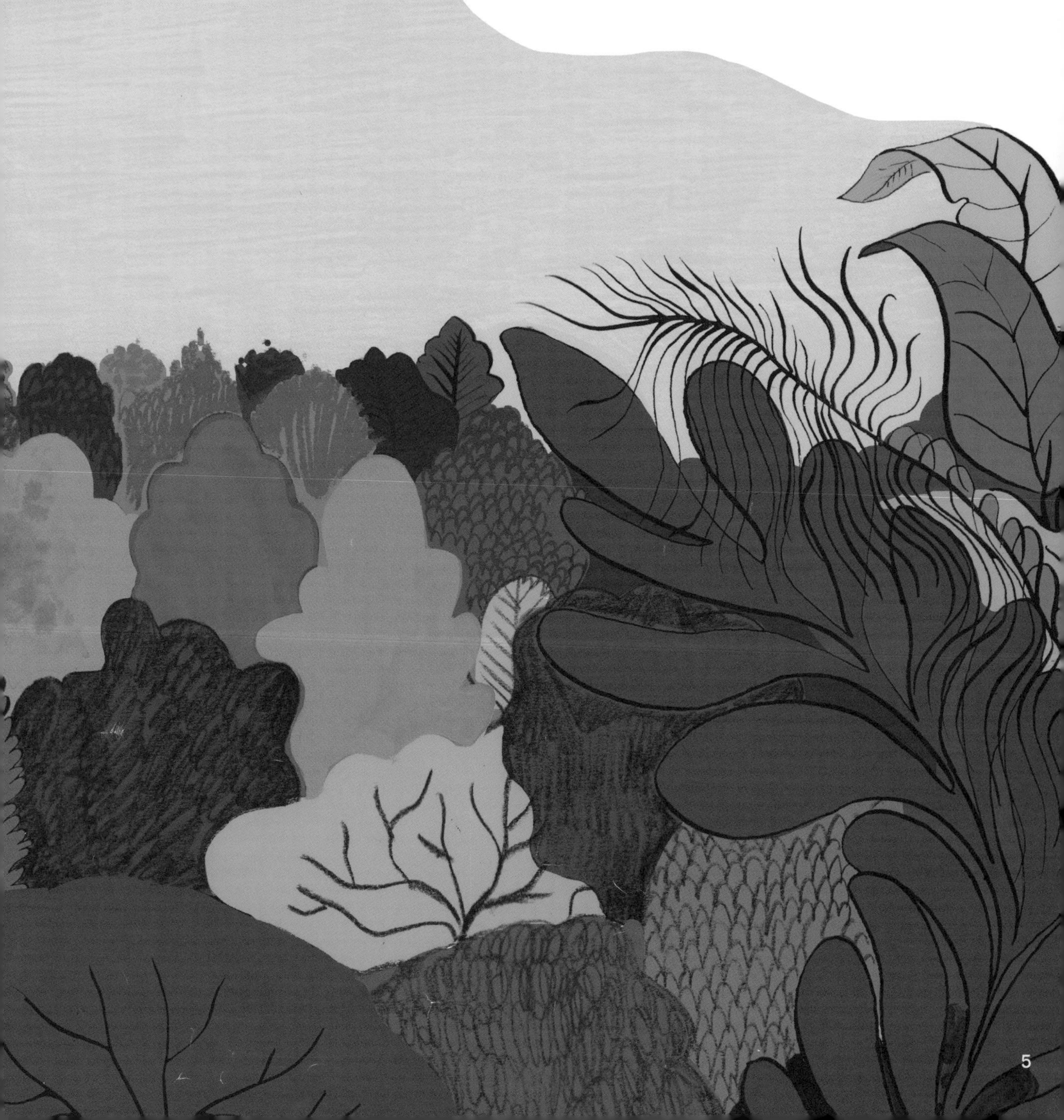

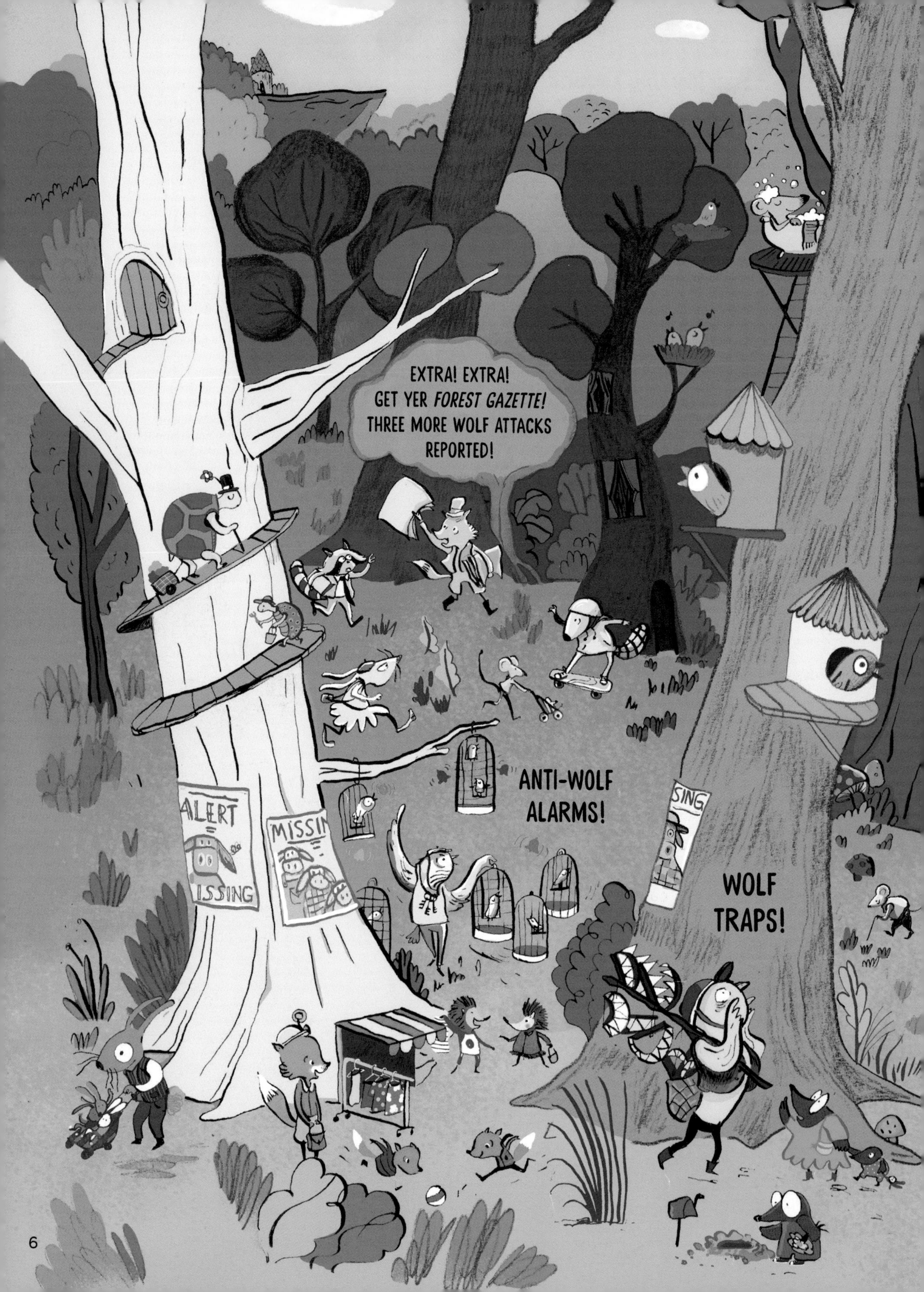
EXTRA! EXTRA!
GET YER *FOREST GAZETTE!*
THREE MORE WOLF ATTACKS
REPORTED!
ANTI-WOLF
ALARMS!
WOLF
TRAPS!
ALERT
ISSING
MISSIN
SING

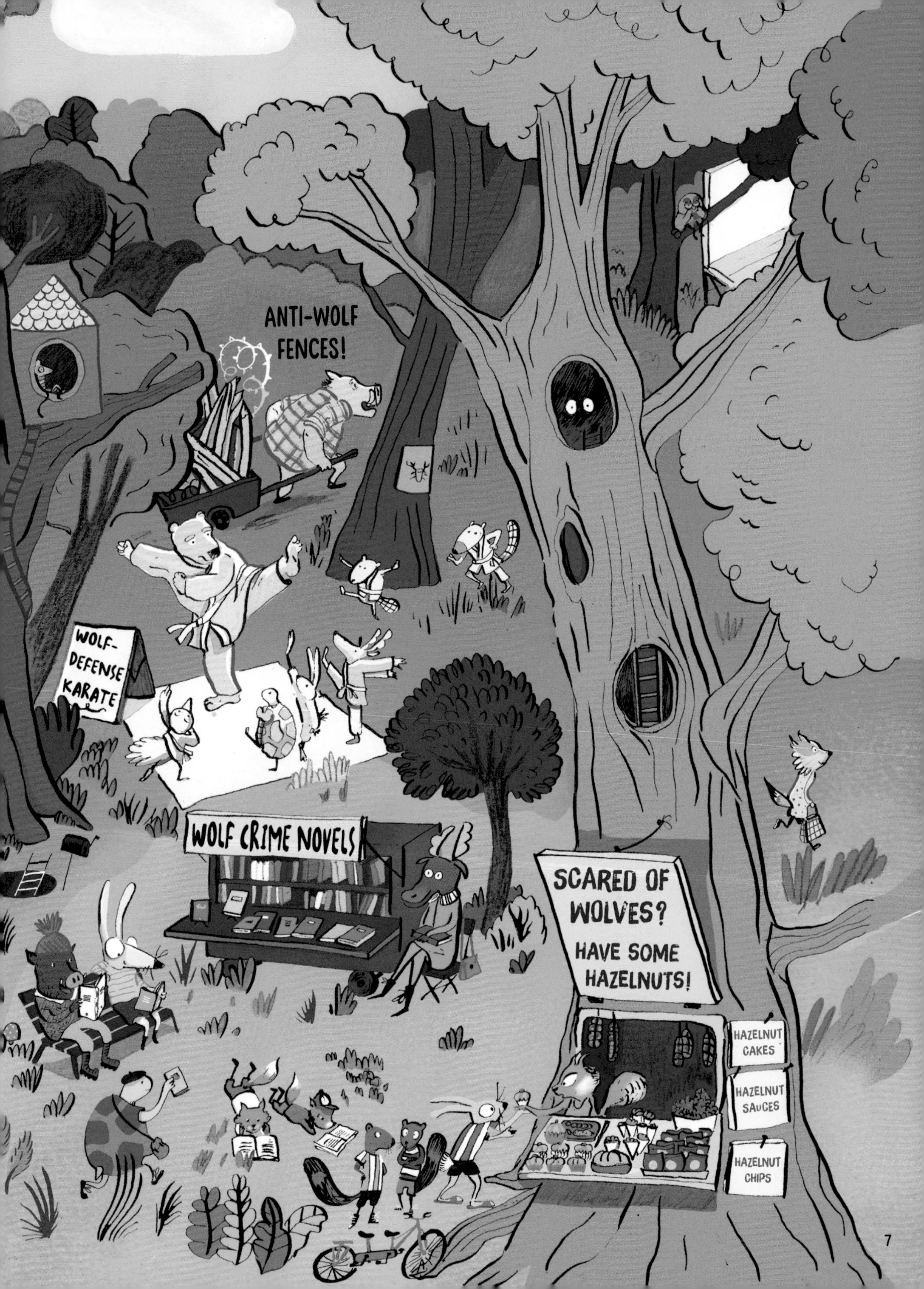
ANTI-WOLF FENCES!
WOLF-DEFENSE KARATE
WOLF CRIME NOVELS
SCARED OF WOLVES?
HAVE SOME HAZELNUTS!
HAZELNUT CAKES
HAZELNUT SAUCES
HAZELNUT CHIPS

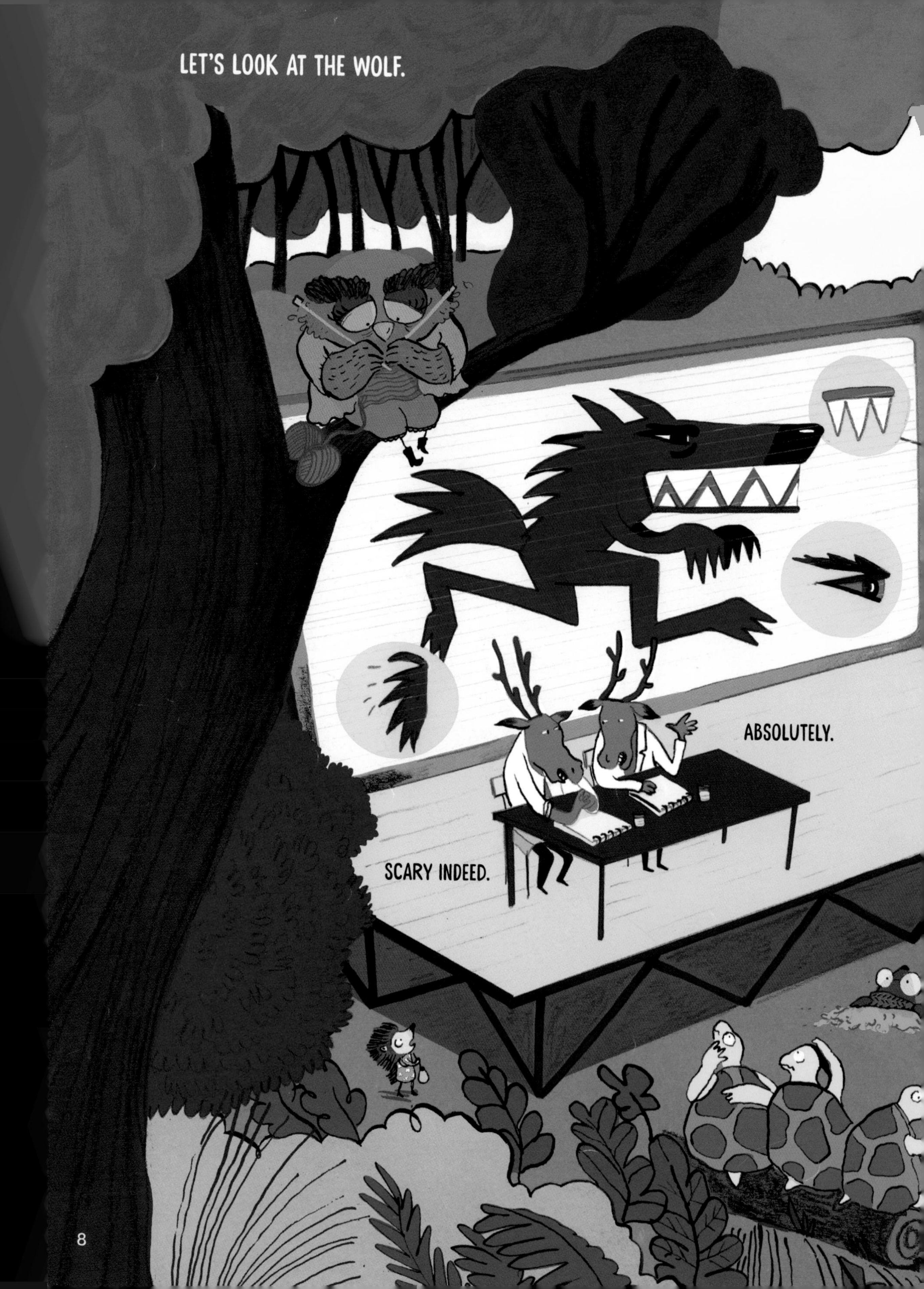
LET'S LOOK AT THE WOLF.
ABSOLUTELY.
SCARY INDEED.

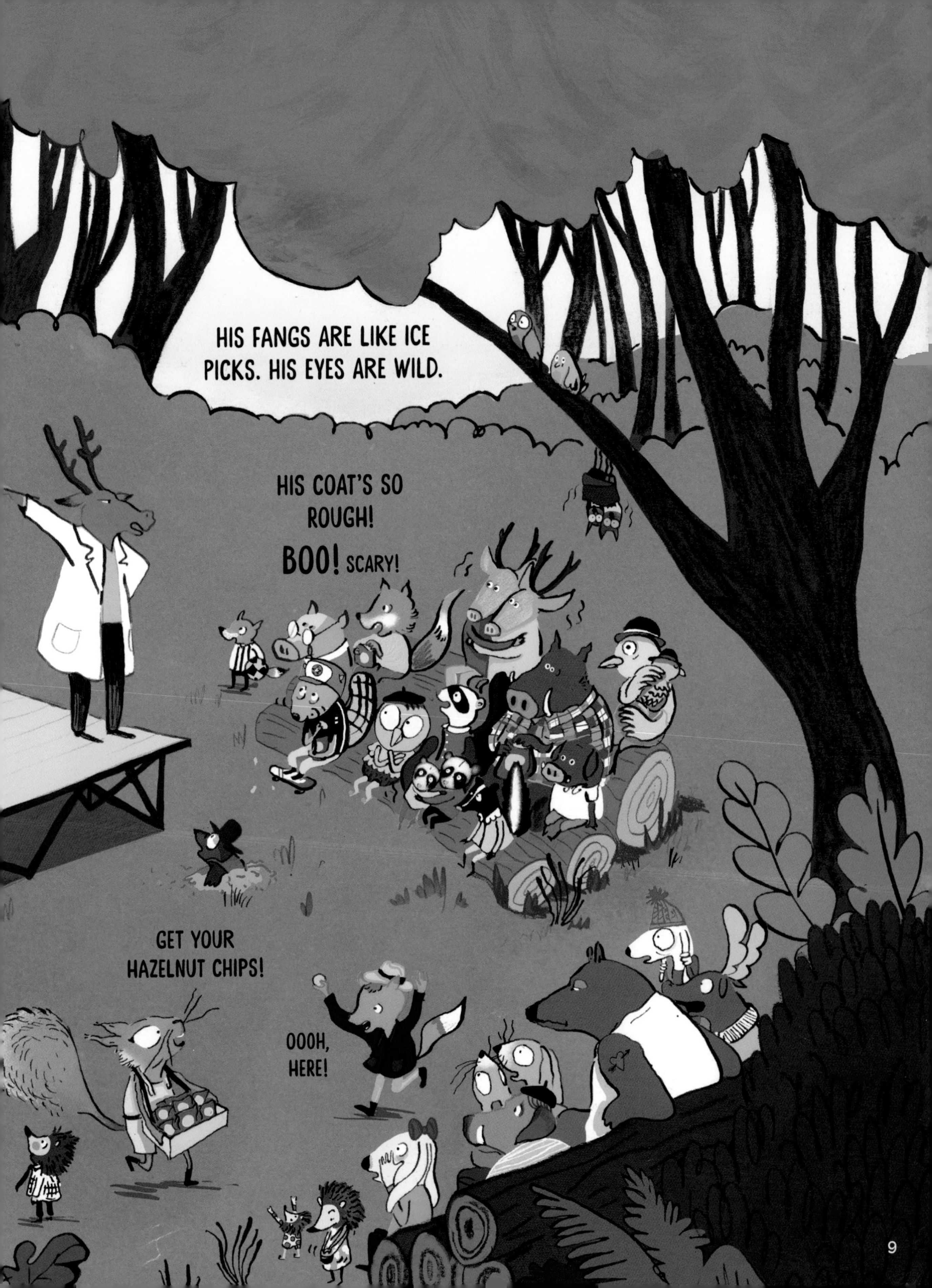
HIS FANGS ARE LIKE ICE PICKS. HIS EYES ARE WILD.
HIS COAT'S SO ROUGH!
BOO! SCARY!
GET YOUR HAZELNUT CHIPS!
OOOH, HERE!

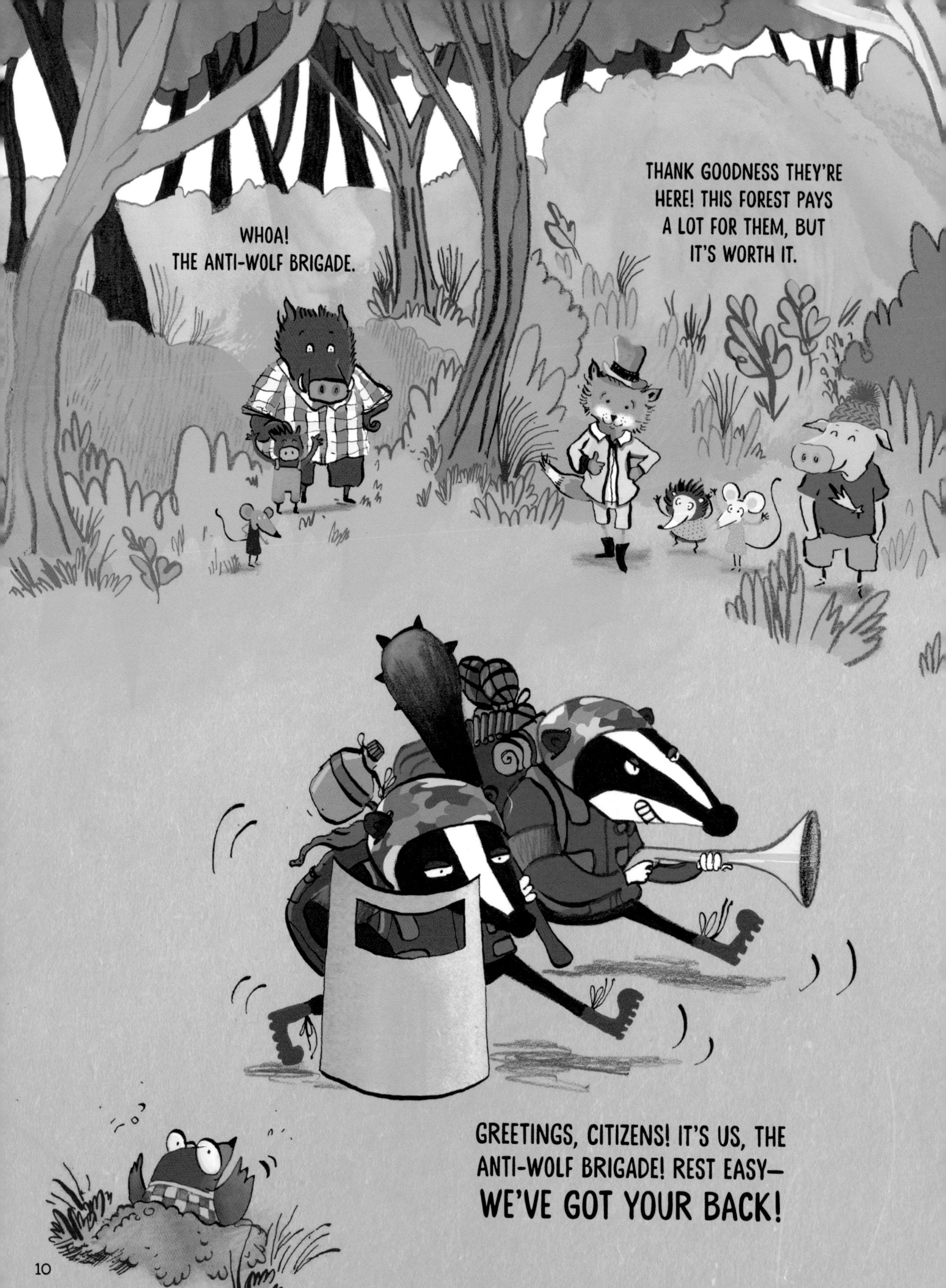
WHOA!
THE ANTI-WOLF BRIGADE.
THANK GOODNESS THEY'RE HERE! THIS FOREST PAYS A LOT FOR THEM, BUT IT'S WORTH IT.
GREETINGS, CITIZENS! IT'S US, THE ANTI-WOLF BRIGADE! REST EASY—
WE'VE GOT YOUR BACK!

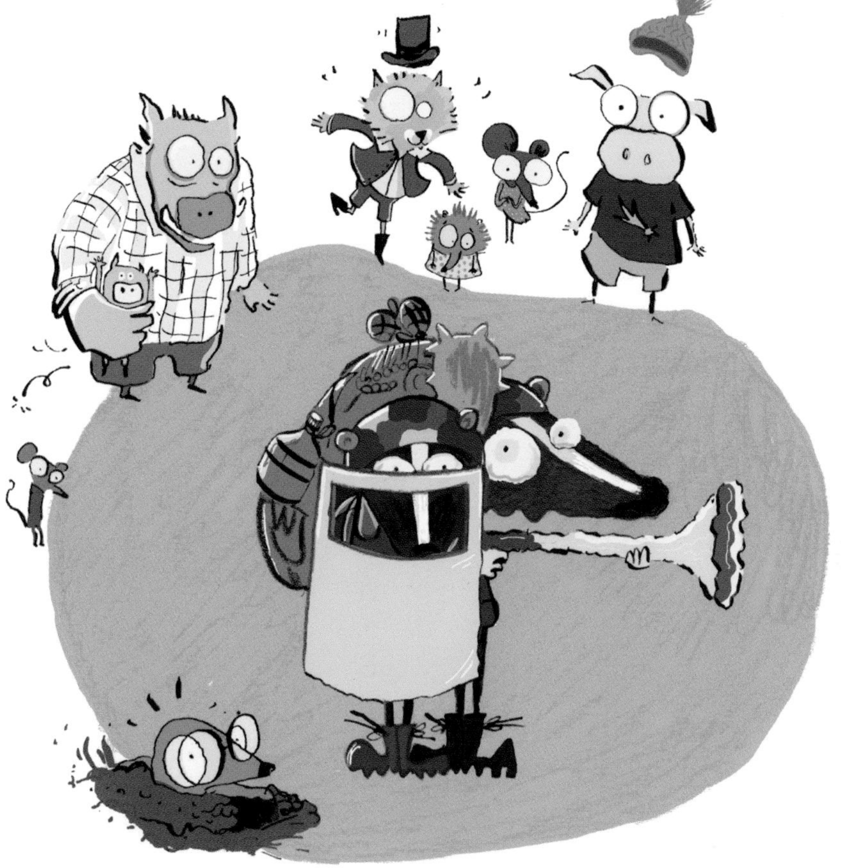

HERE COMES THE WOLF!!!

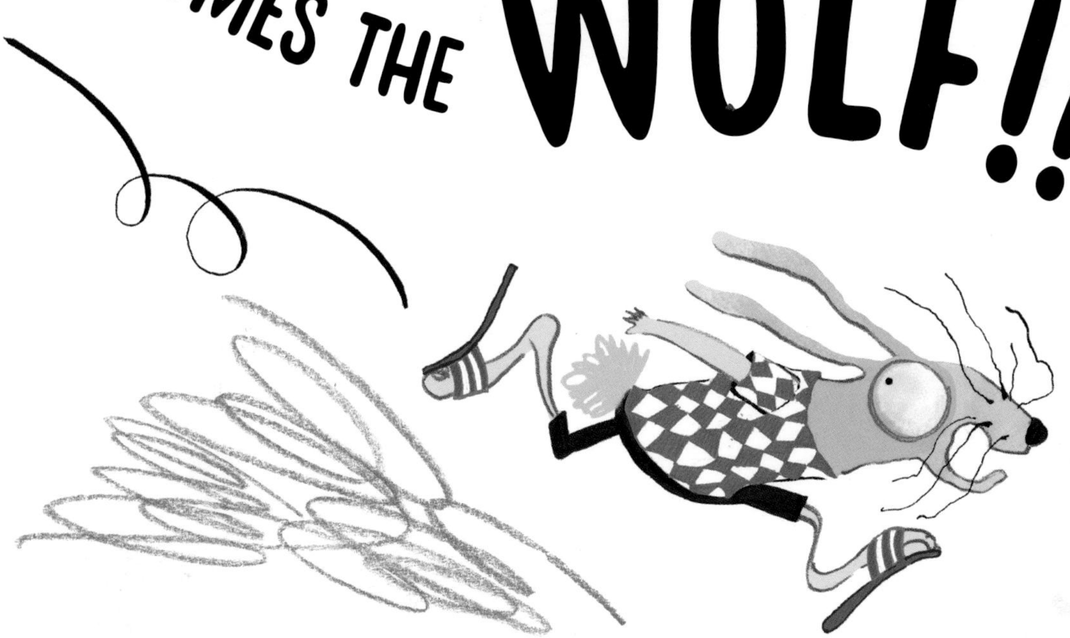

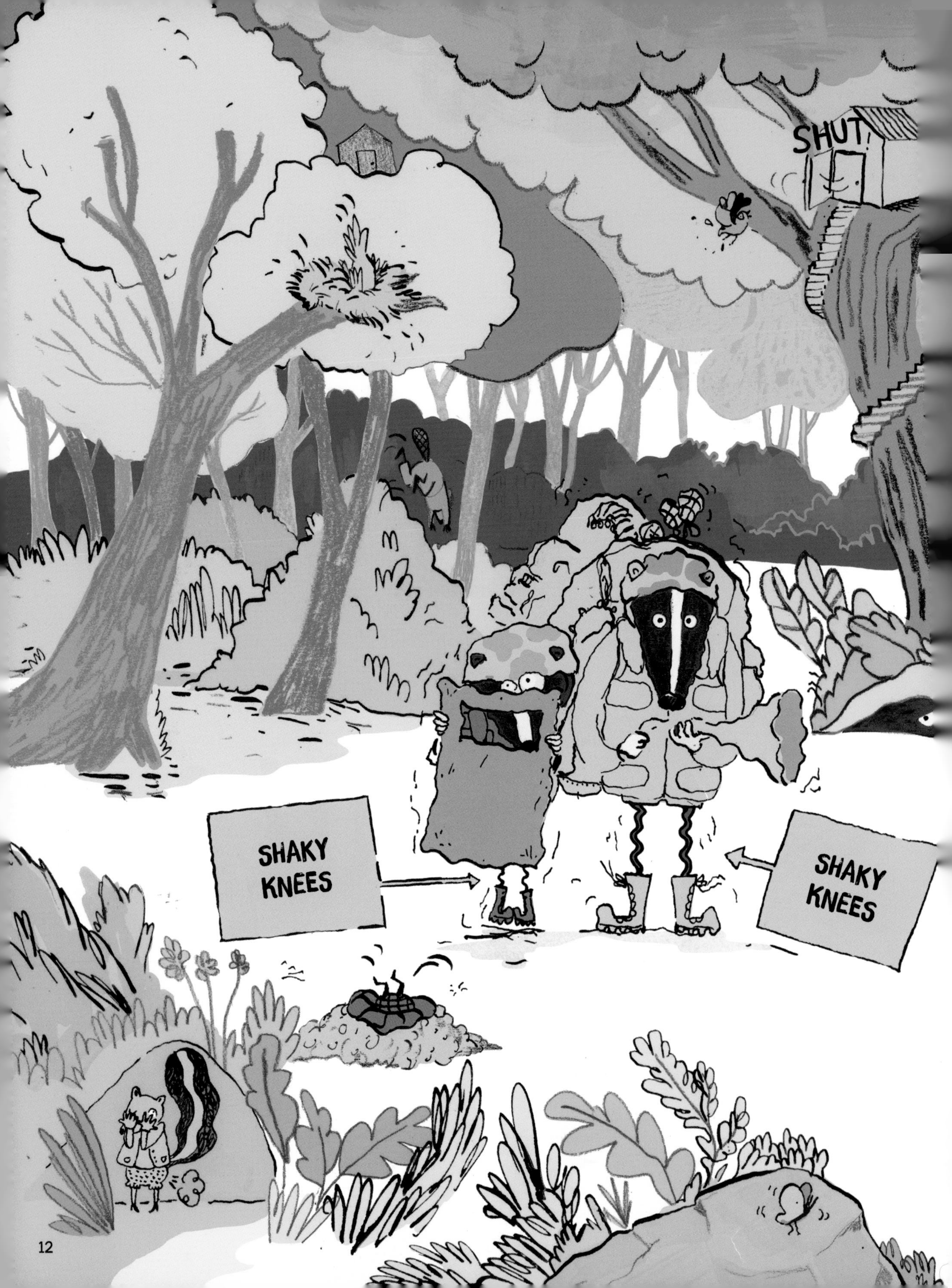
SHUT!
SHAKY KNEES
SHAKY KNEES

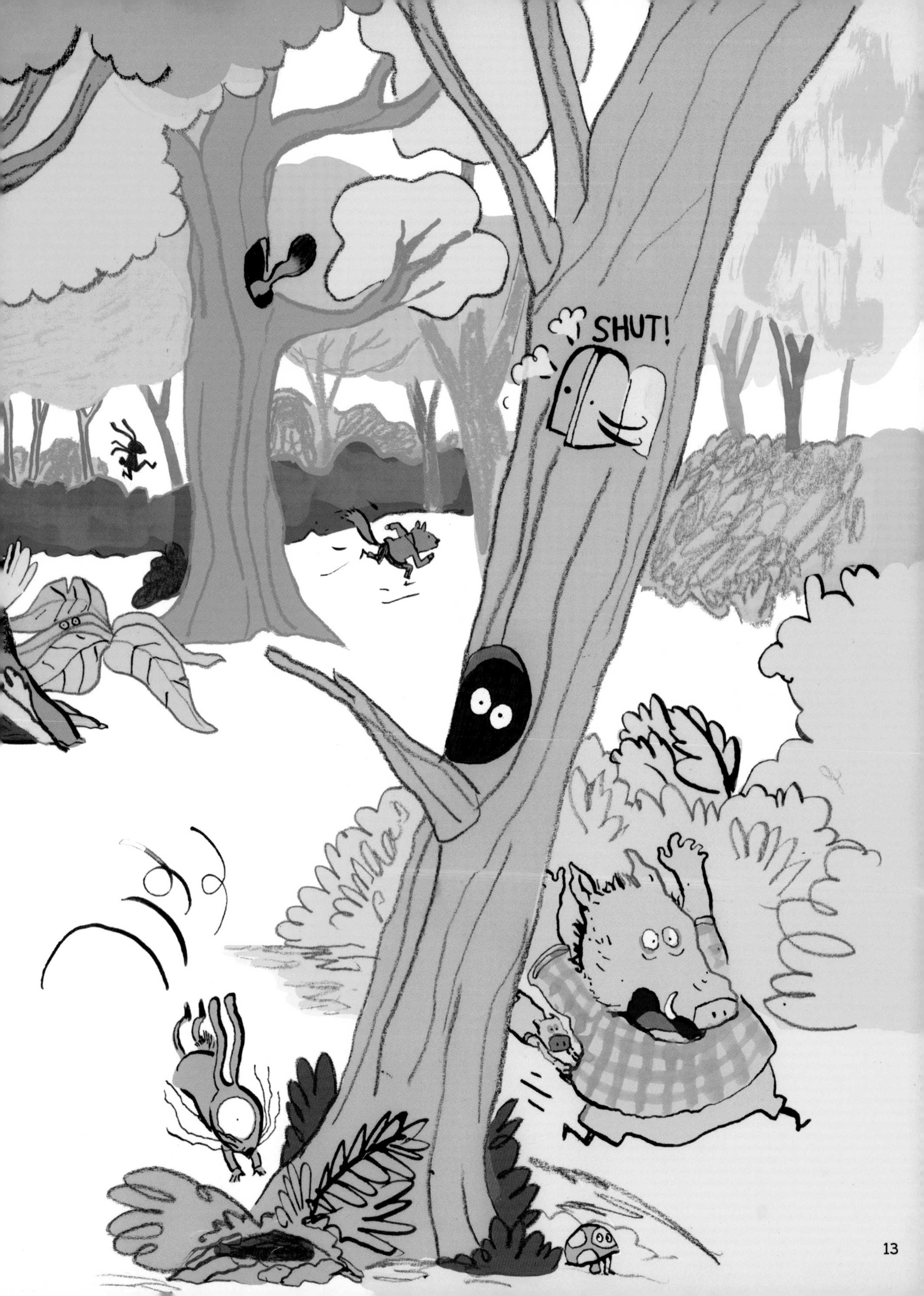
SHUT!

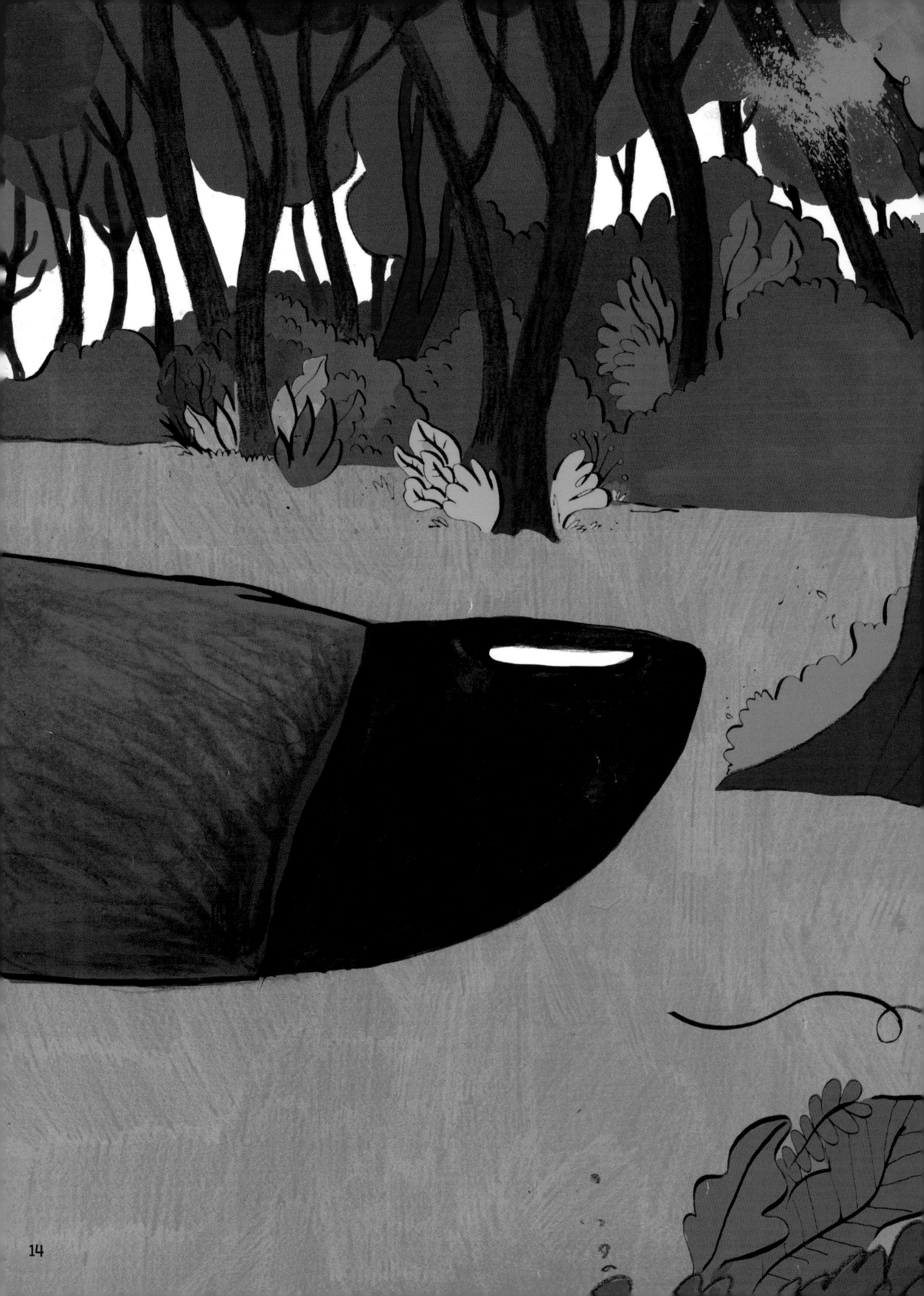

I THINK I SAW HIS SNOUT!
I HEAR HE'S GOT HORRIBLE FANGS INSIDE . . .
AND MEAN, MAD EYES UP TOP . . .

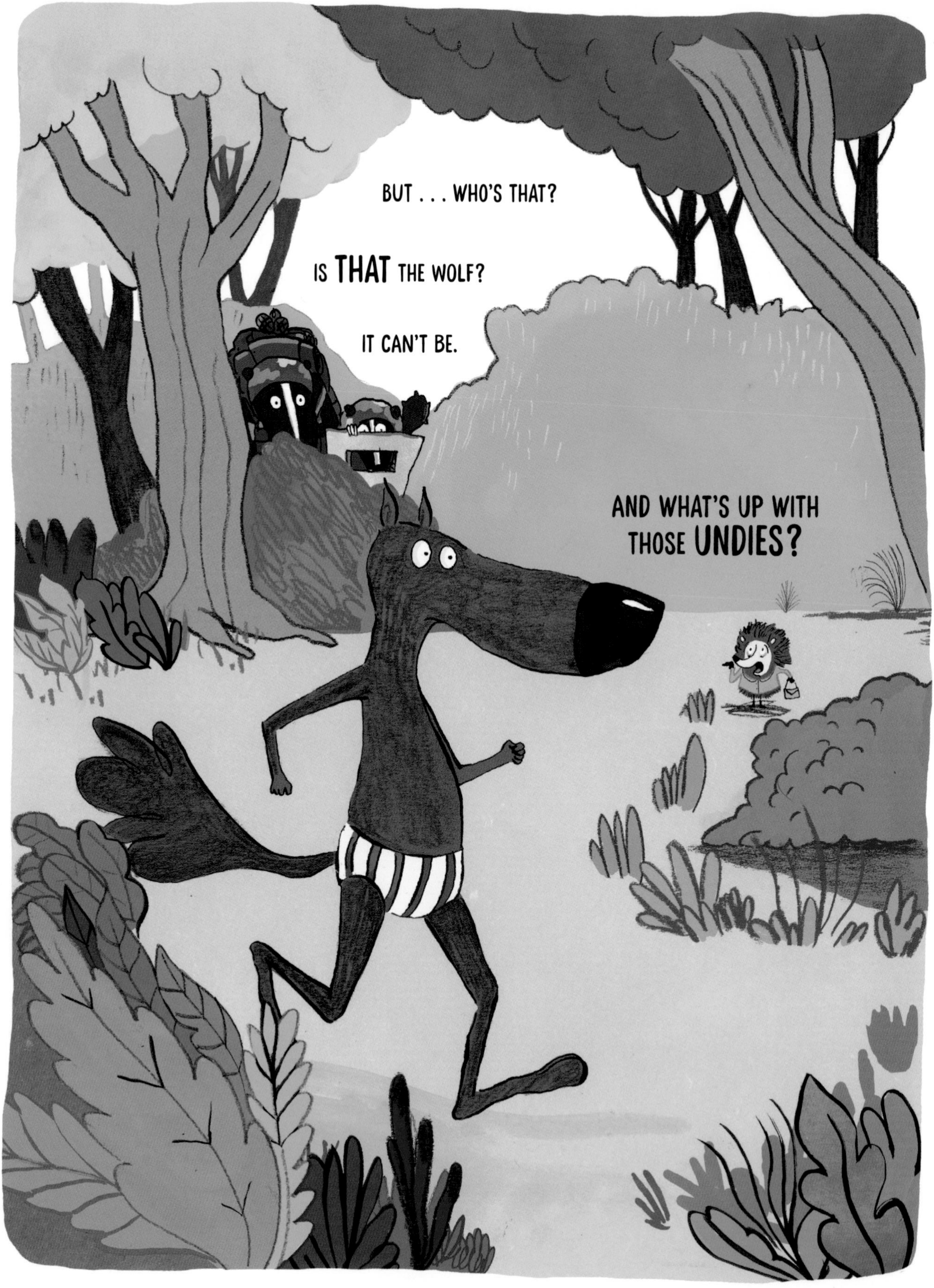
BUT . . . WHO'S THAT?
IS THAT THE WOLF?
IT CAN'T BE.
AND WHAT'S UP WITH THOSE UNDIES?

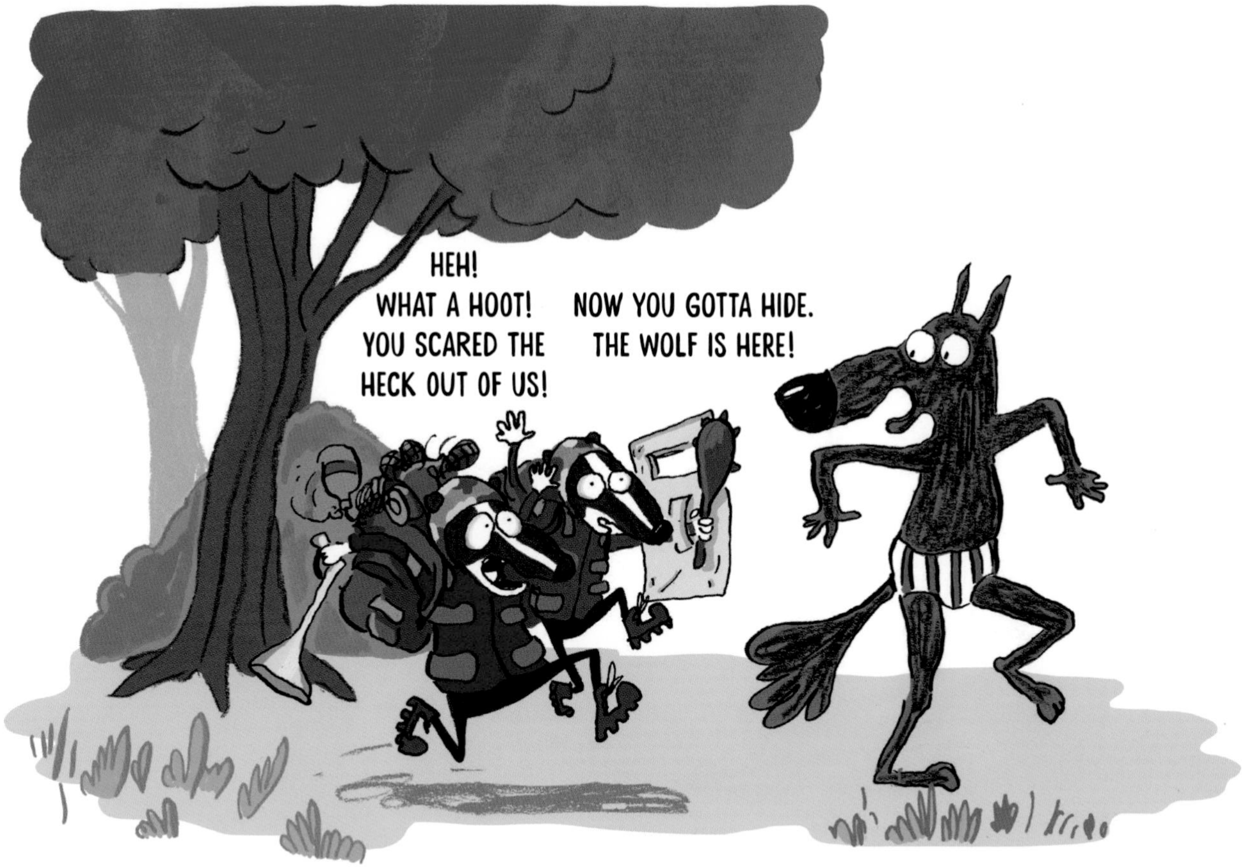
HEH!
WHAT A HOOT!
YOU SCARED THE
HECK OUT OF US!
NOW YOU GOTTA HIDE.
THE WOLF IS HERE!

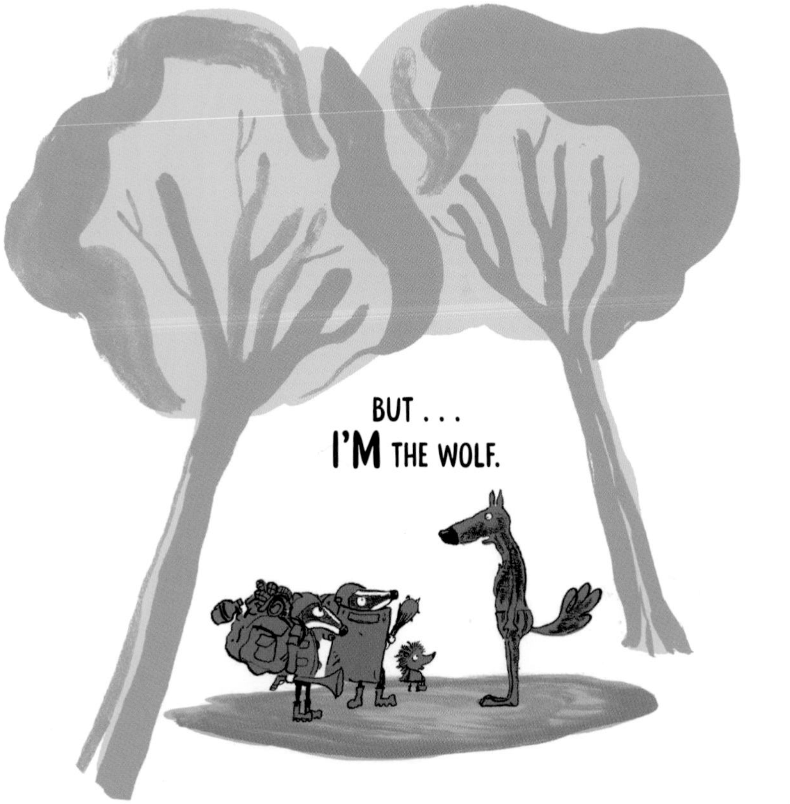
BUT . . .
I'M THE WOLF.

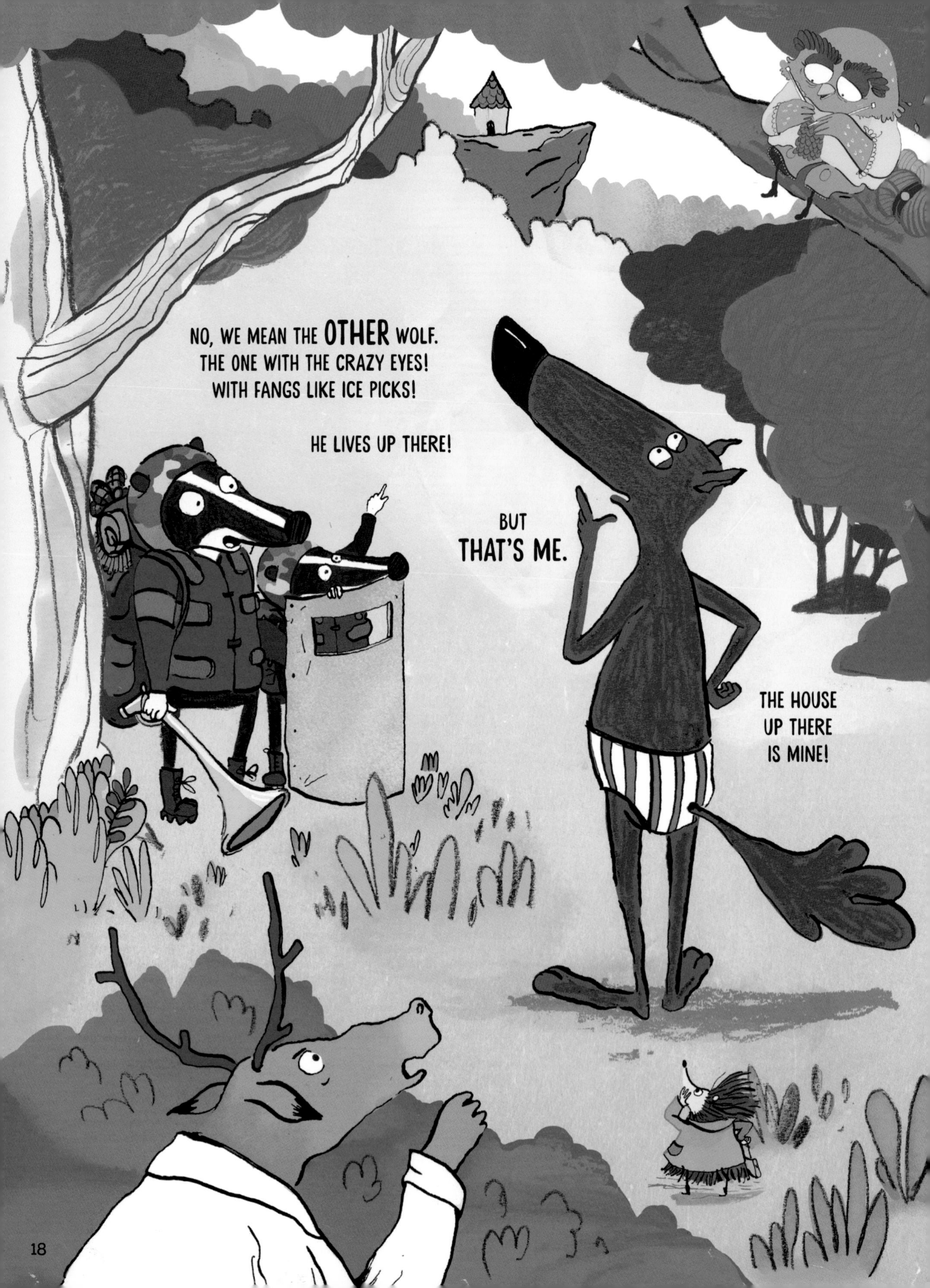
NO, WE MEAN THE OTHER WOLF. THE ONE WITH THE CRAZY EYES! WITH FANGS LIKE ICE PICKS!
HE LIVES UP THERE!
BUT THAT'S ME.
THE HOUSE UP THERE IS MINE!

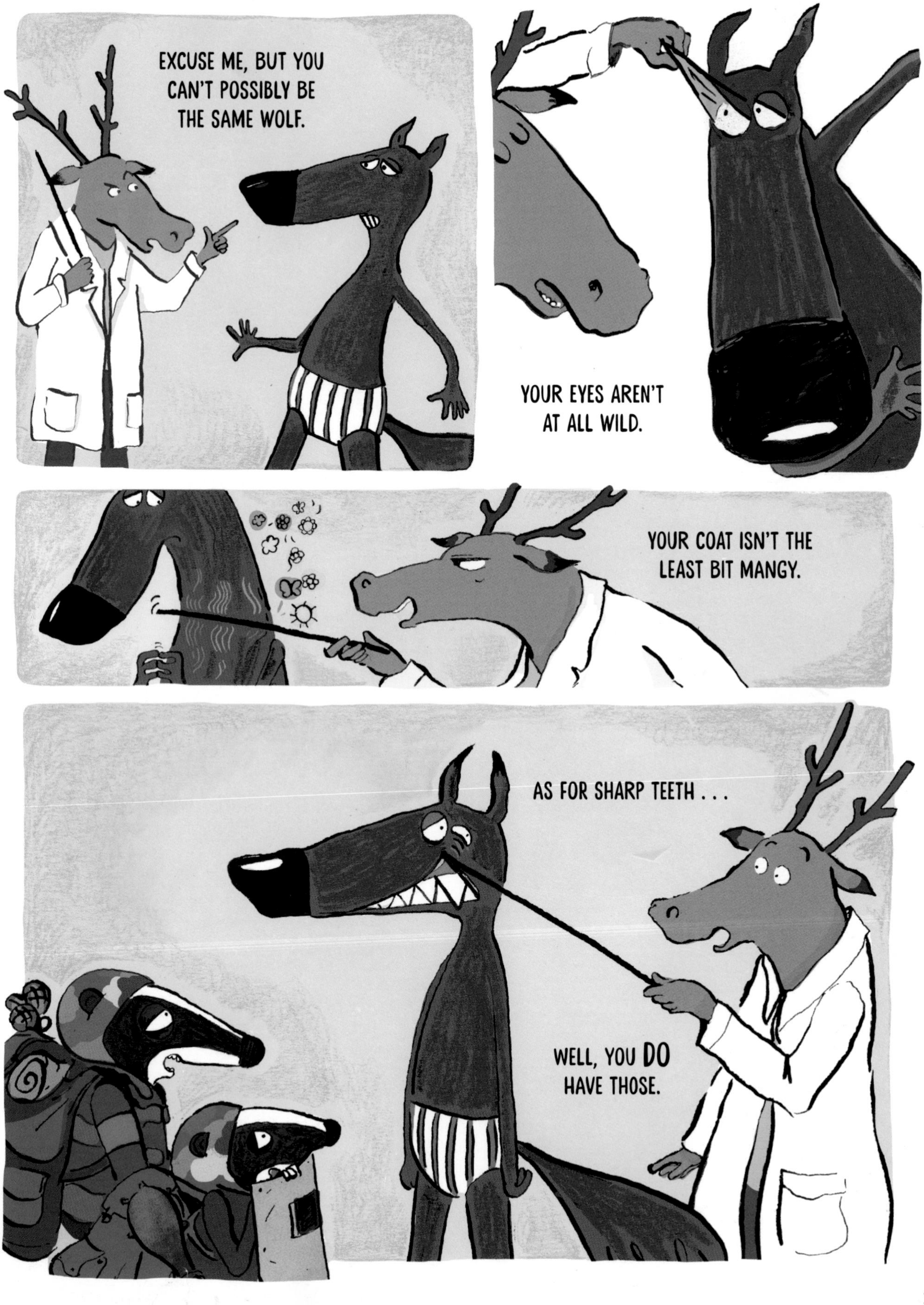
EXCUSE ME, BUT YOU CAN'T POSSIBLY BE THE SAME WOLF.
YOUR EYES AREN'T AT ALL WILD.
YOUR COAT ISN'T THE LEAST BIT MANGY.
AS FOR SHARP TEETH . . .
WELL, YOU **DO** HAVE THOSE.

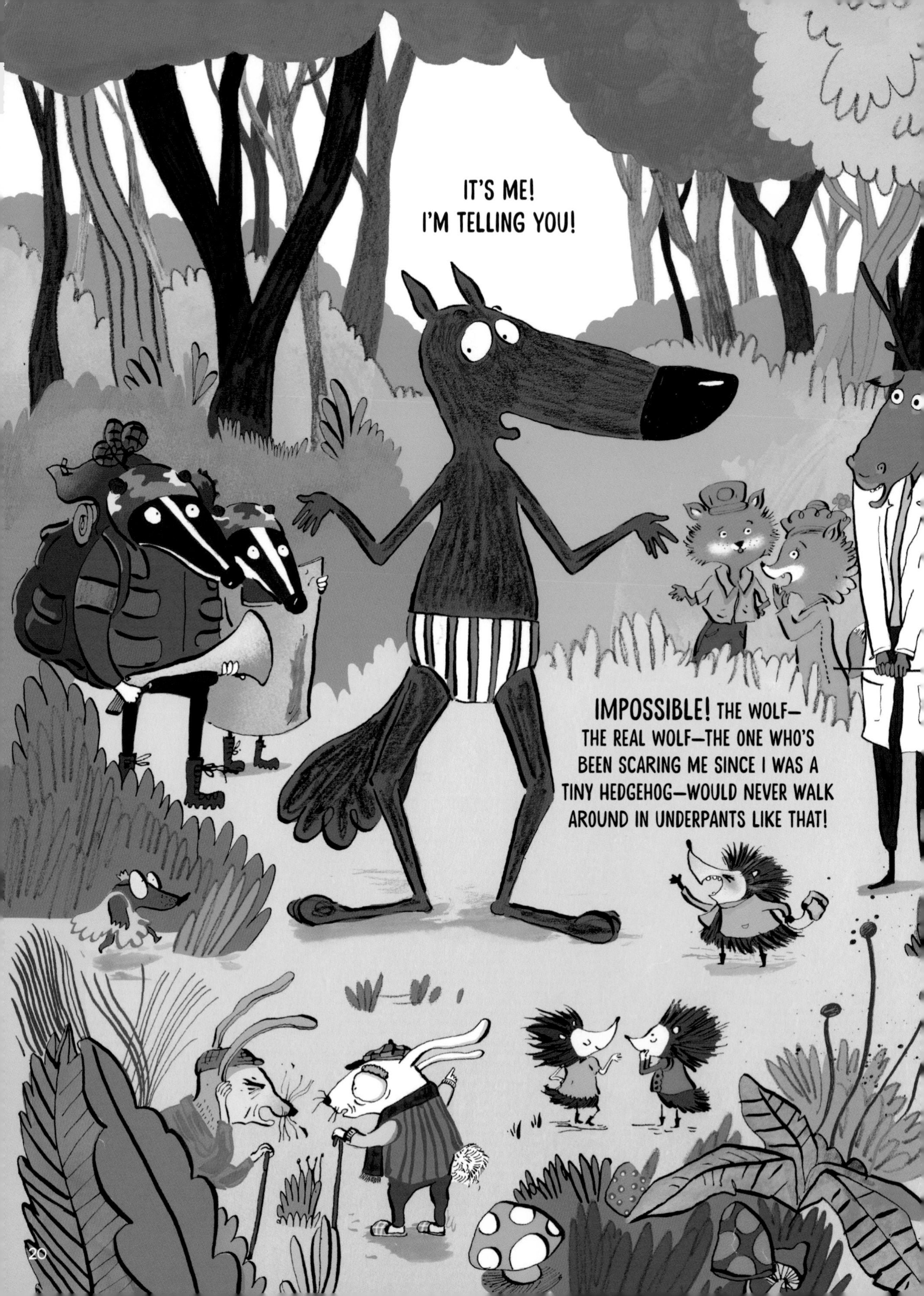
IT'S ME!
I'M TELLING YOU!
IMPOSSIBLE! THE WOLF—
THE REAL WOLF—THE ONE WHO'S
BEEN SCARING ME SINCE I WAS A
TINY HEDGEHOG—WOULD NEVER WALK
AROUND IN UNDERPANTS LIKE THAT!

OH, THESE
UNDERPANTS?

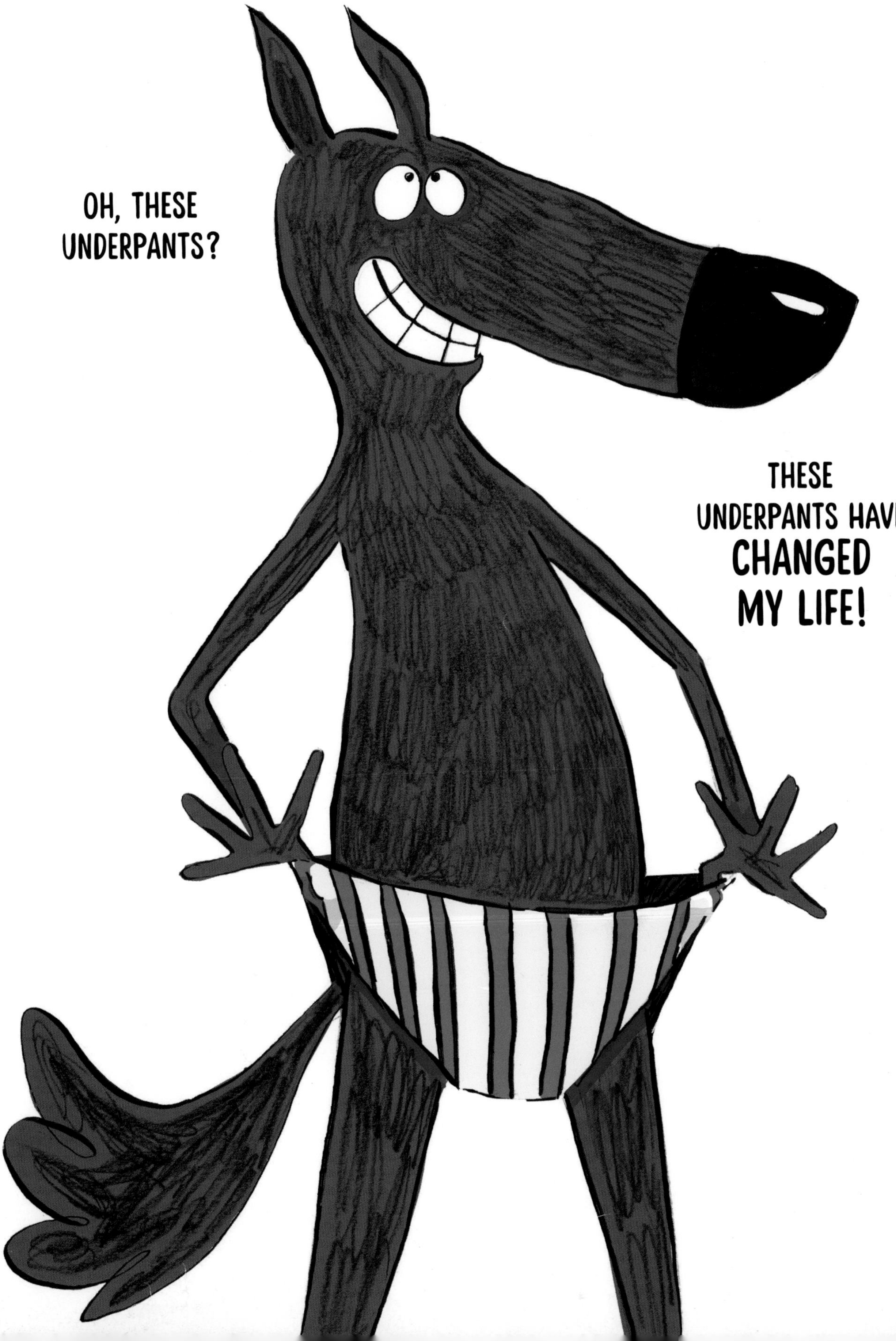

THESE
UNDERPANTS HAVE
**CHANGED
MY LIFE!**

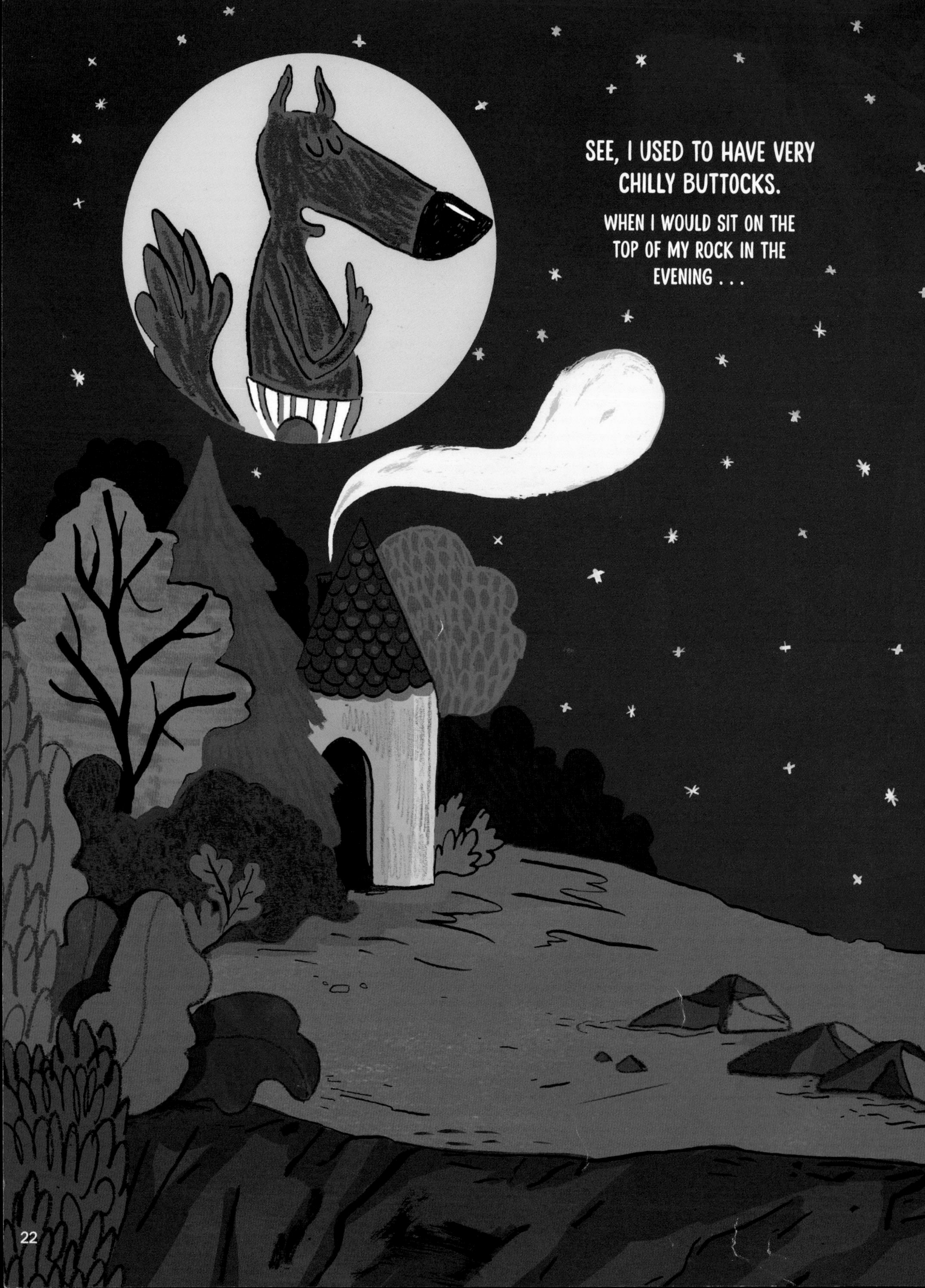
SEE, I USED TO HAVE VERY CHILLY BUTTOCKS.
WHEN I WOULD SIT ON THE TOP OF MY ROCK IN THE EVENING . . .

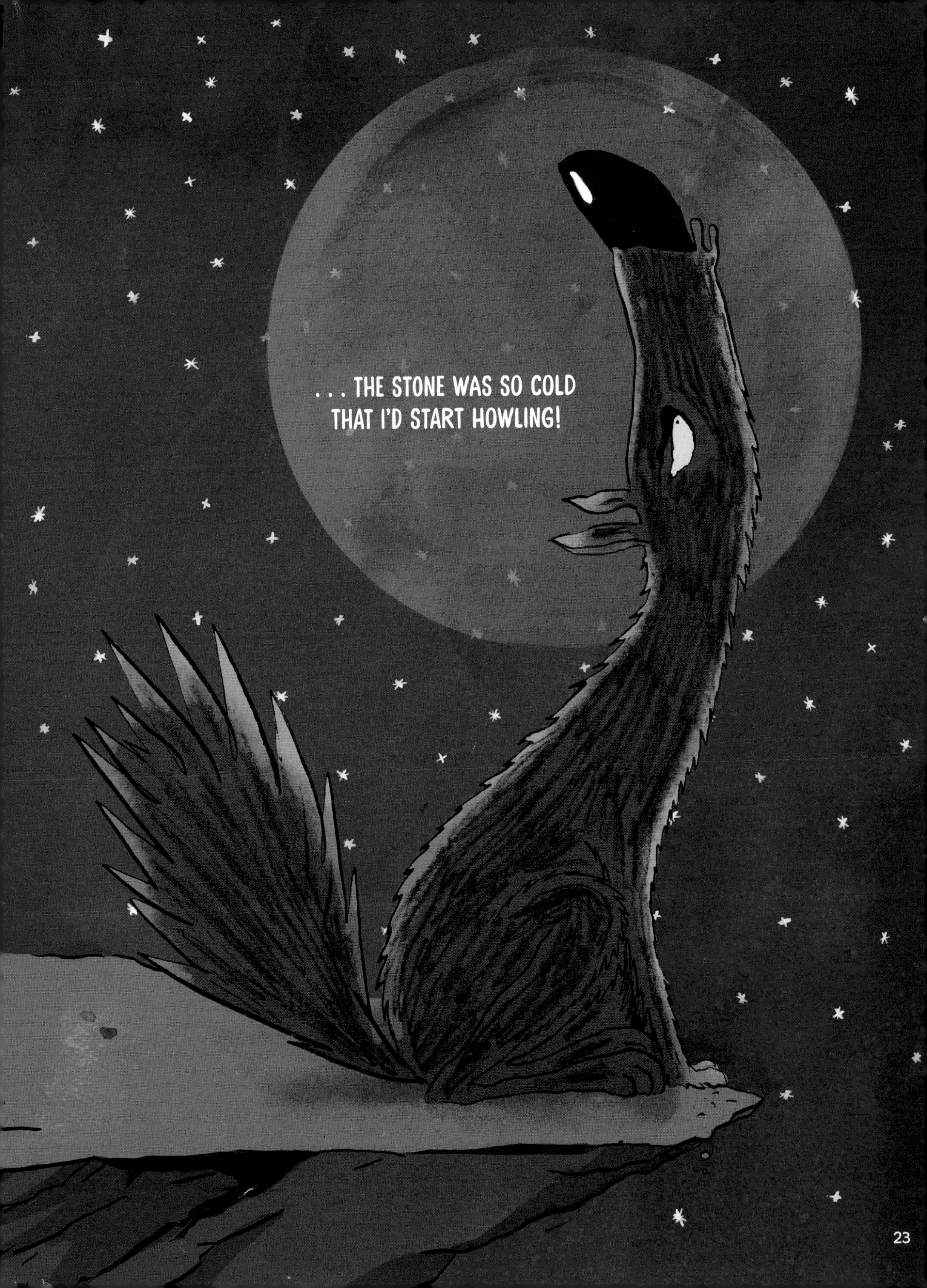
. . . THE STONE WAS SO COLD
THAT I'D START HOWLING!

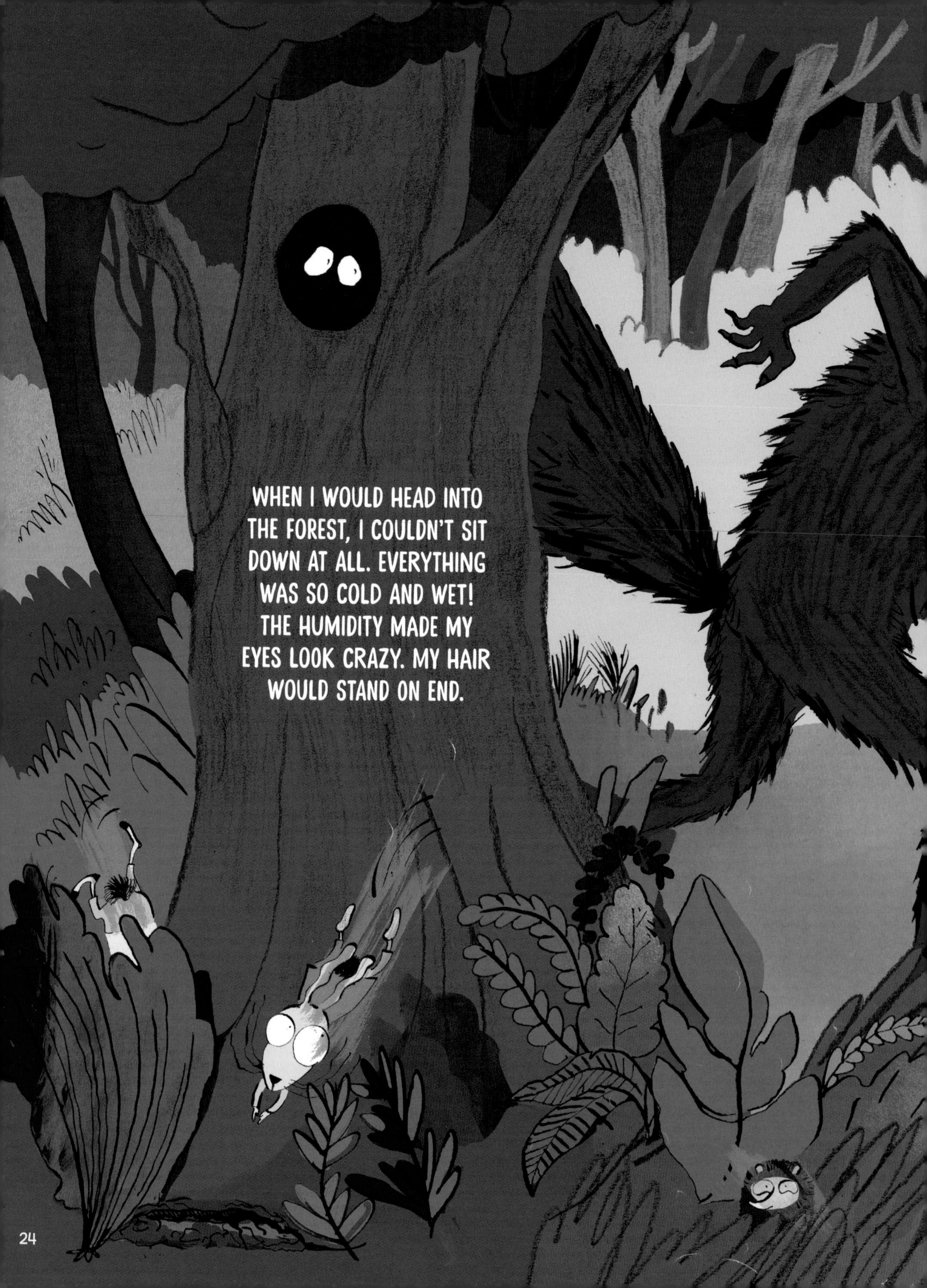
WHEN I WOULD HEAD INTO THE FOREST, I COULDN'T SIT DOWN AT ALL. EVERYTHING WAS SO COLD AND WET! THE HUMIDITY MADE MY EYES LOOK CRAZY. MY HAIR WOULD STAND ON END.

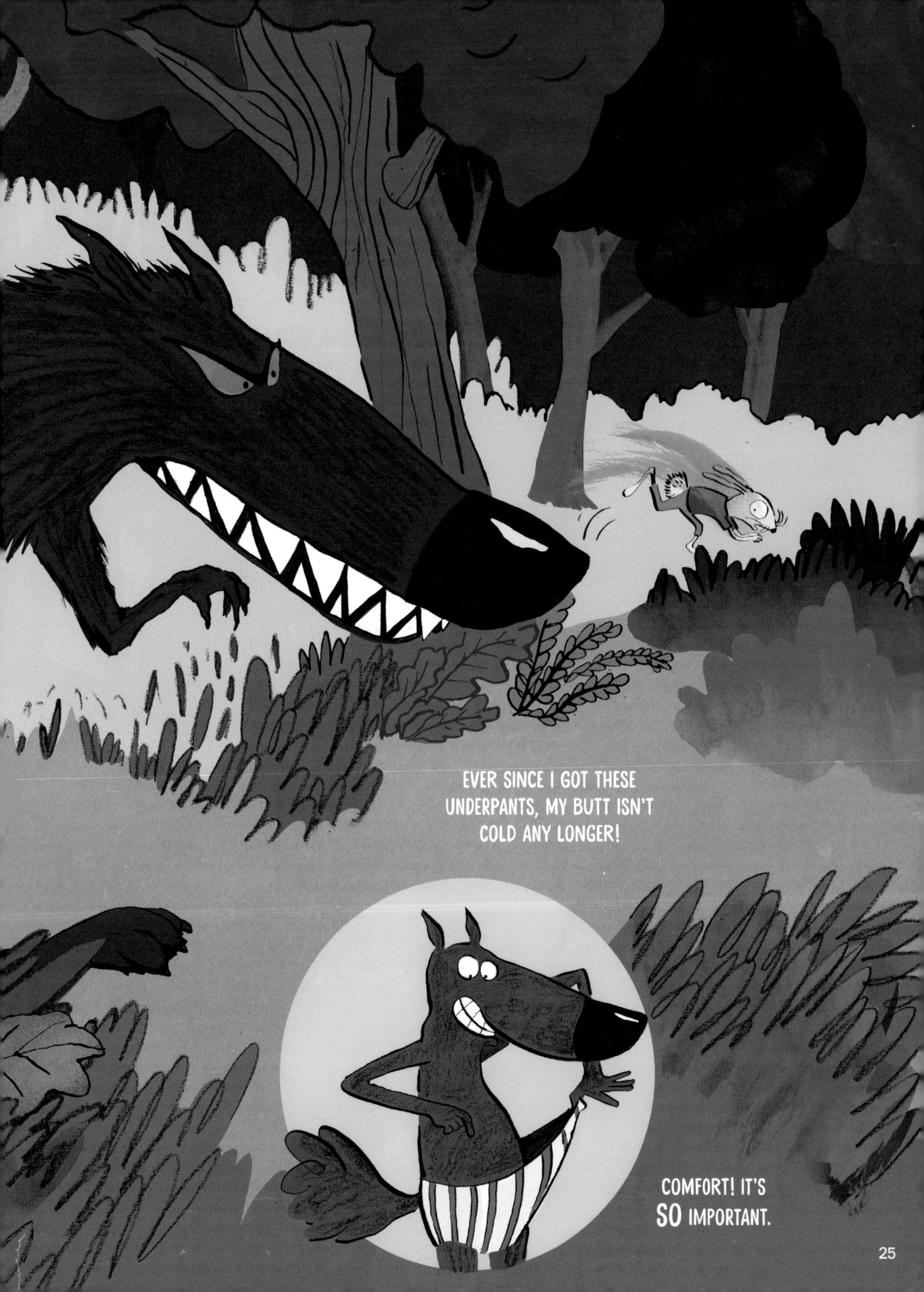
EVER SINCE I GOT THESE
UNDERPANTS, MY BUTT ISN'T
COLD ANY LONGER!
COMFORT! IT'S
SO IMPORTANT.

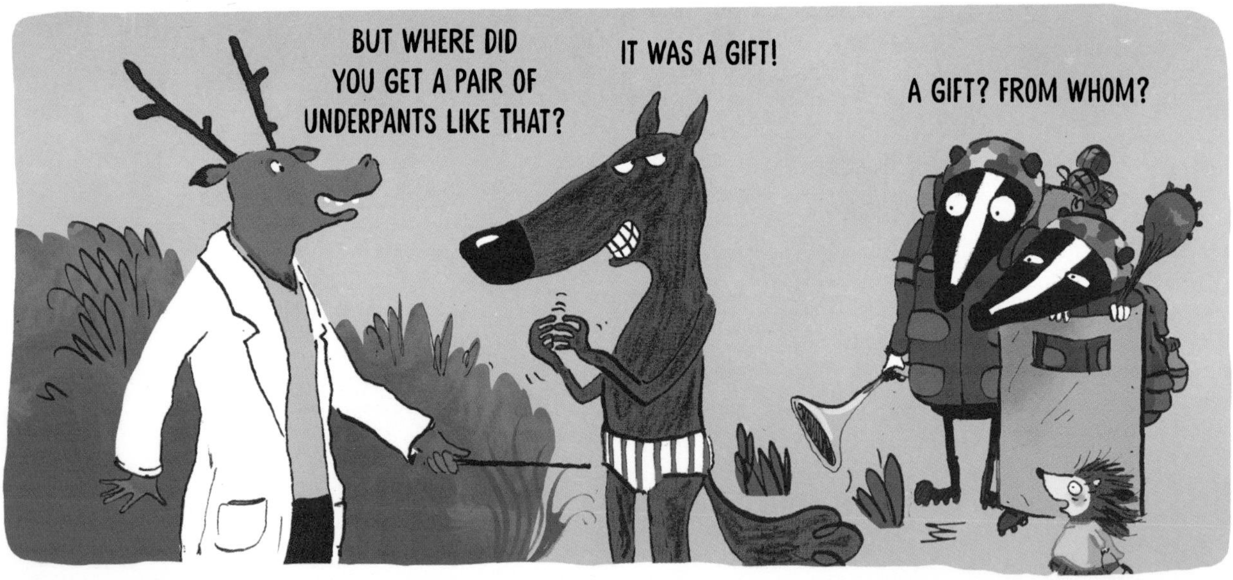
BUT WHERE DID YOU GET A PAIR OF UNDERPANTS LIKE THAT?
IT WAS A GIFT!
A GIFT? FROM WHOM?

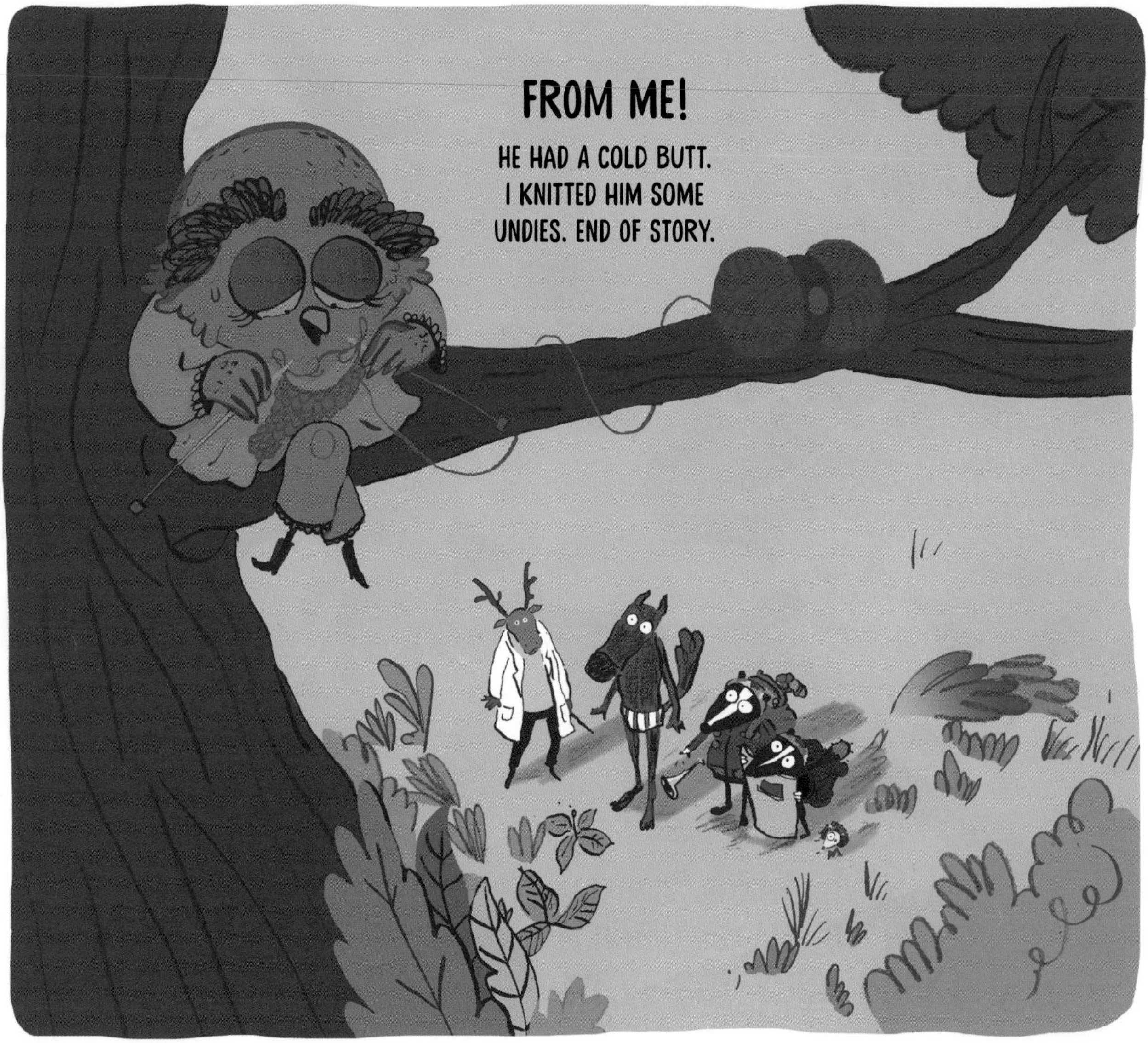
FROM ME!
HE HAD A COLD BUTT. I KNITTED HIM SOME UNDIES. END OF STORY.

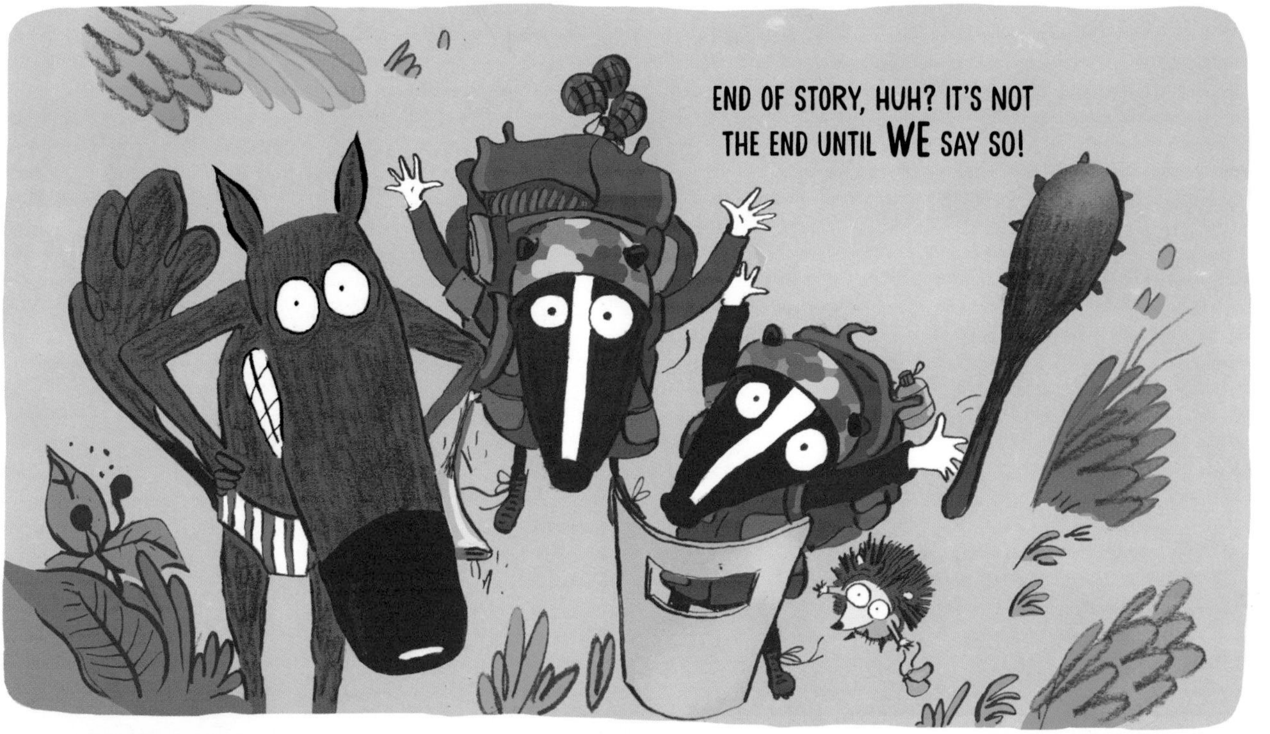
END OF STORY, HUH? IT'S NOT THE END UNTIL WE SAY SO!

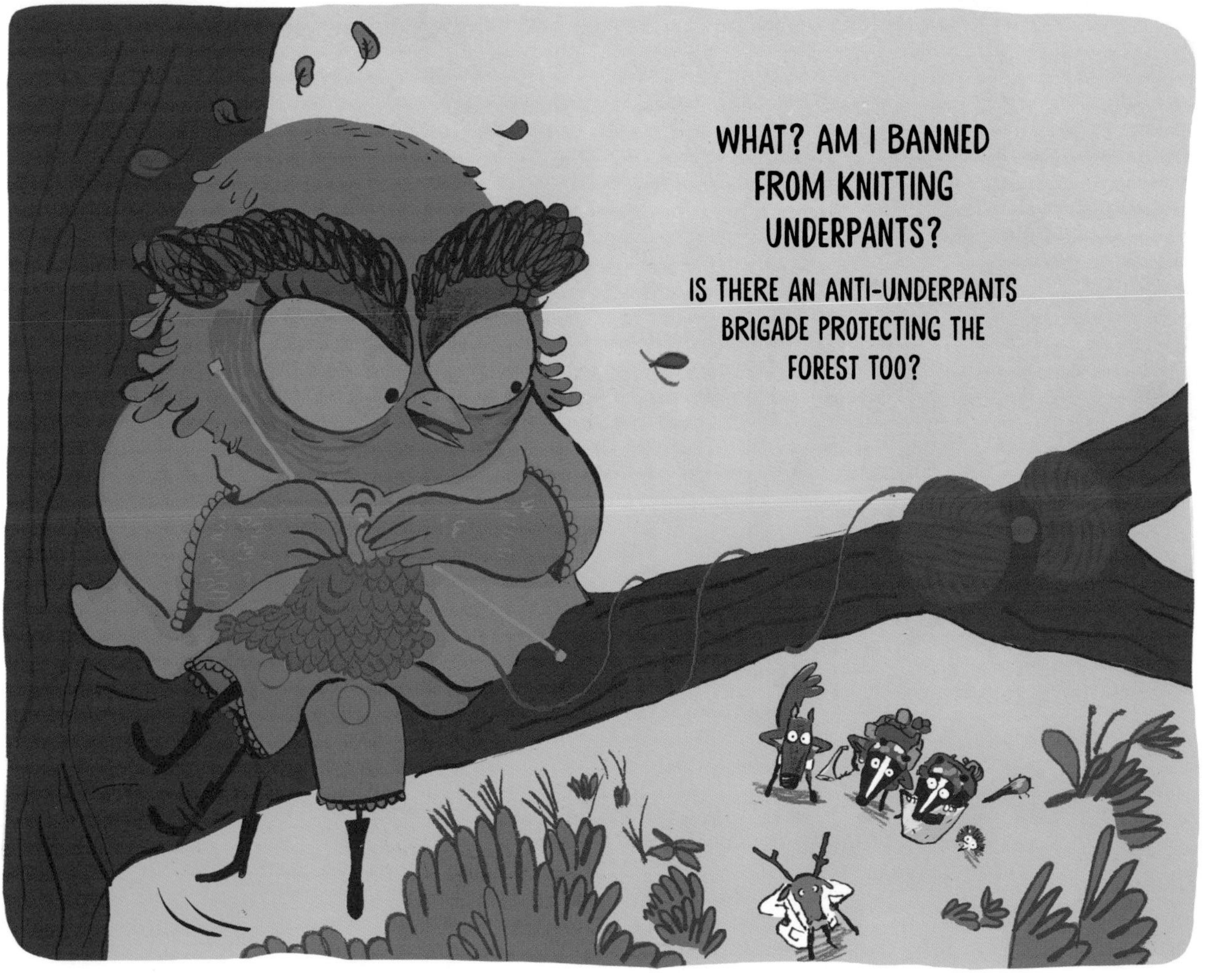
WHAT? AM I BANNED FROM KNITTING UNDERPANTS?
IS THERE AN ANTI-UNDERPANTS BRIGADE PROTECTING THE FOREST TOO?

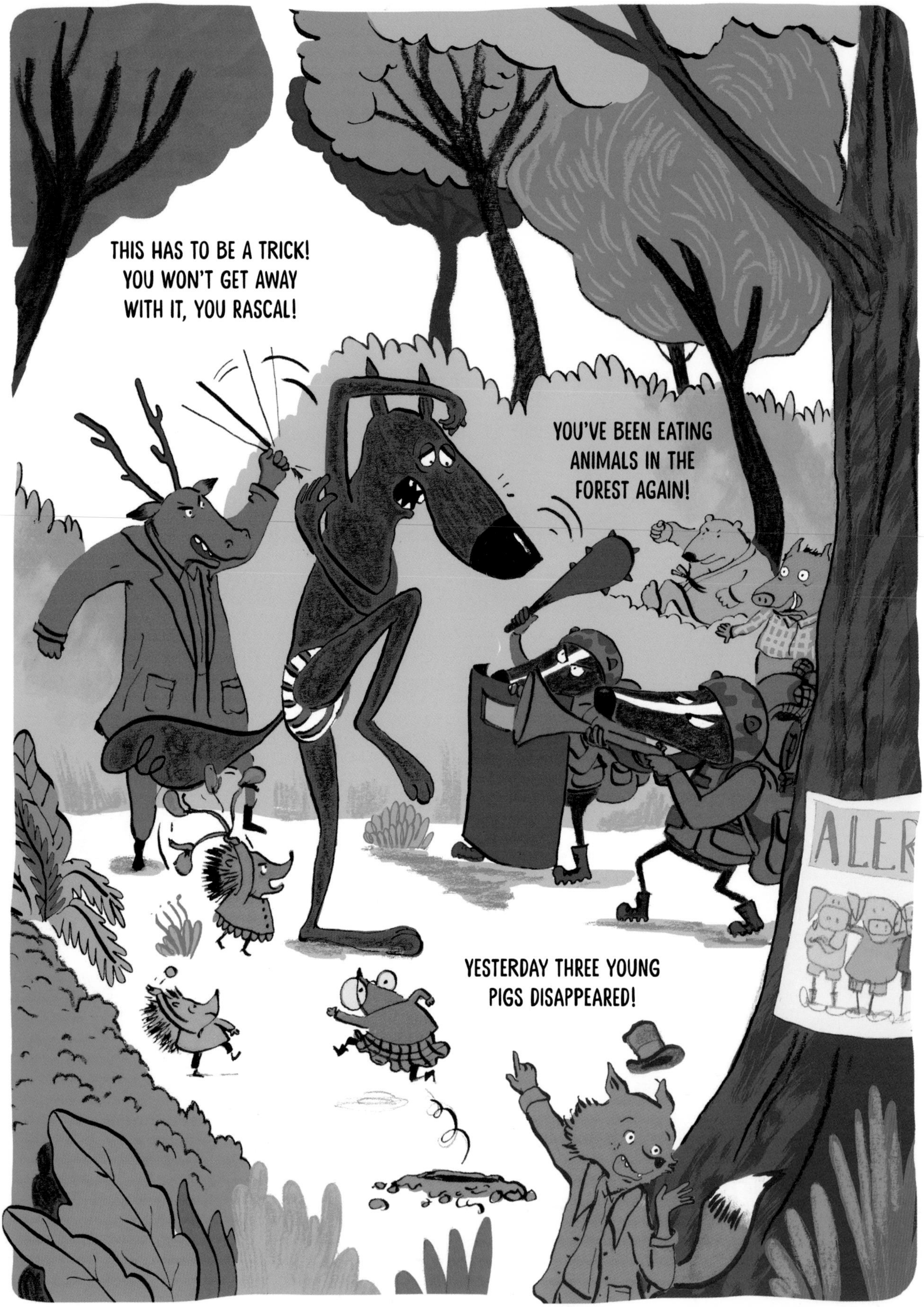
THIS HAS TO BE A TRICK! YOU WON'T GET AWAY WITH IT, YOU RASCAL!
YOU'VE BEEN EATING ANIMALS IN THE FOREST AGAIN!
YESTERDAY THREE YOUNG PIGS DISAPPEARED!

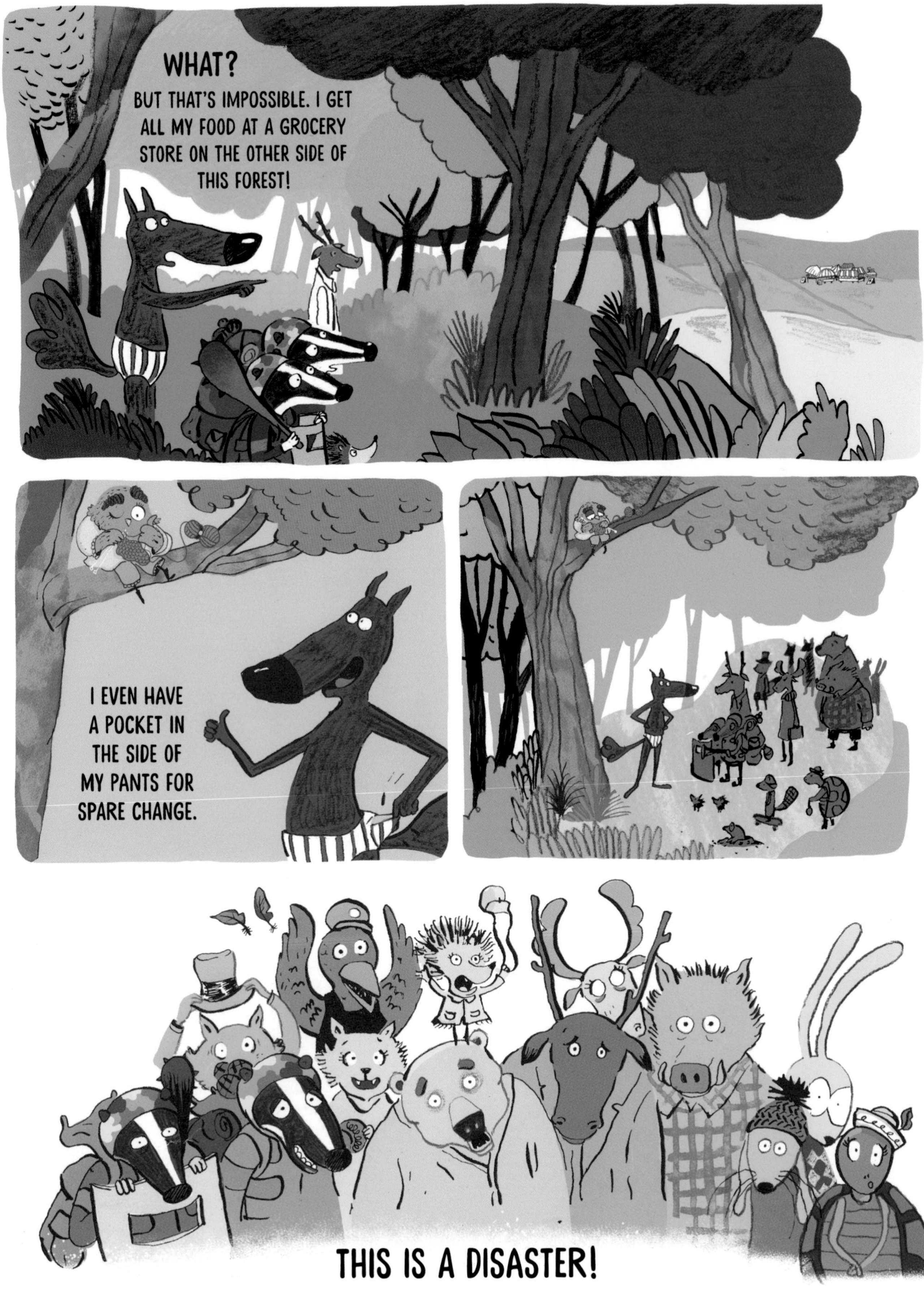
WHAT?
BUT THAT'S IMPOSSIBLE. I GET ALL MY FOOD AT A GROCERY STORE ON THE OTHER SIDE OF THIS FOREST!
I EVEN HAVE A POCKET IN THE SIDE OF MY PANTS FOR SPARE CHANGE.
THIS IS A DISASTER!

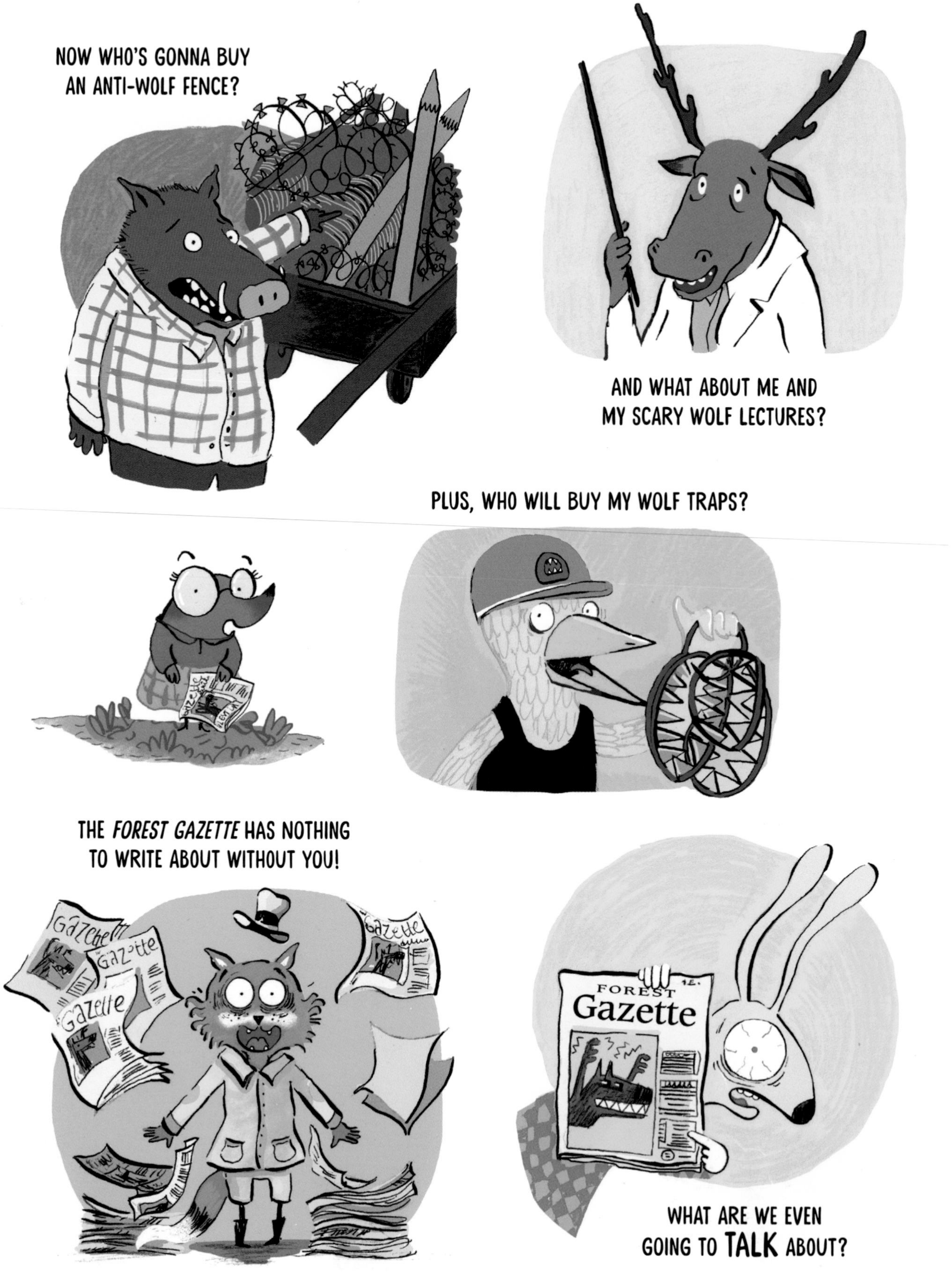
NOW WHO'S GONNA BUY AN ANTI-WOLF FENCE?
AND WHAT ABOUT ME AND MY SCARY WOLF LECTURES?
PLUS, WHO WILL BUY MY WOLF TRAPS?
THE *FOREST GAZETTE* HAS NOTHING TO WRITE ABOUT WITHOUT YOU!
FOREST Gazette
WHAT ARE WE EVEN GOING TO **TALK** ABOUT?

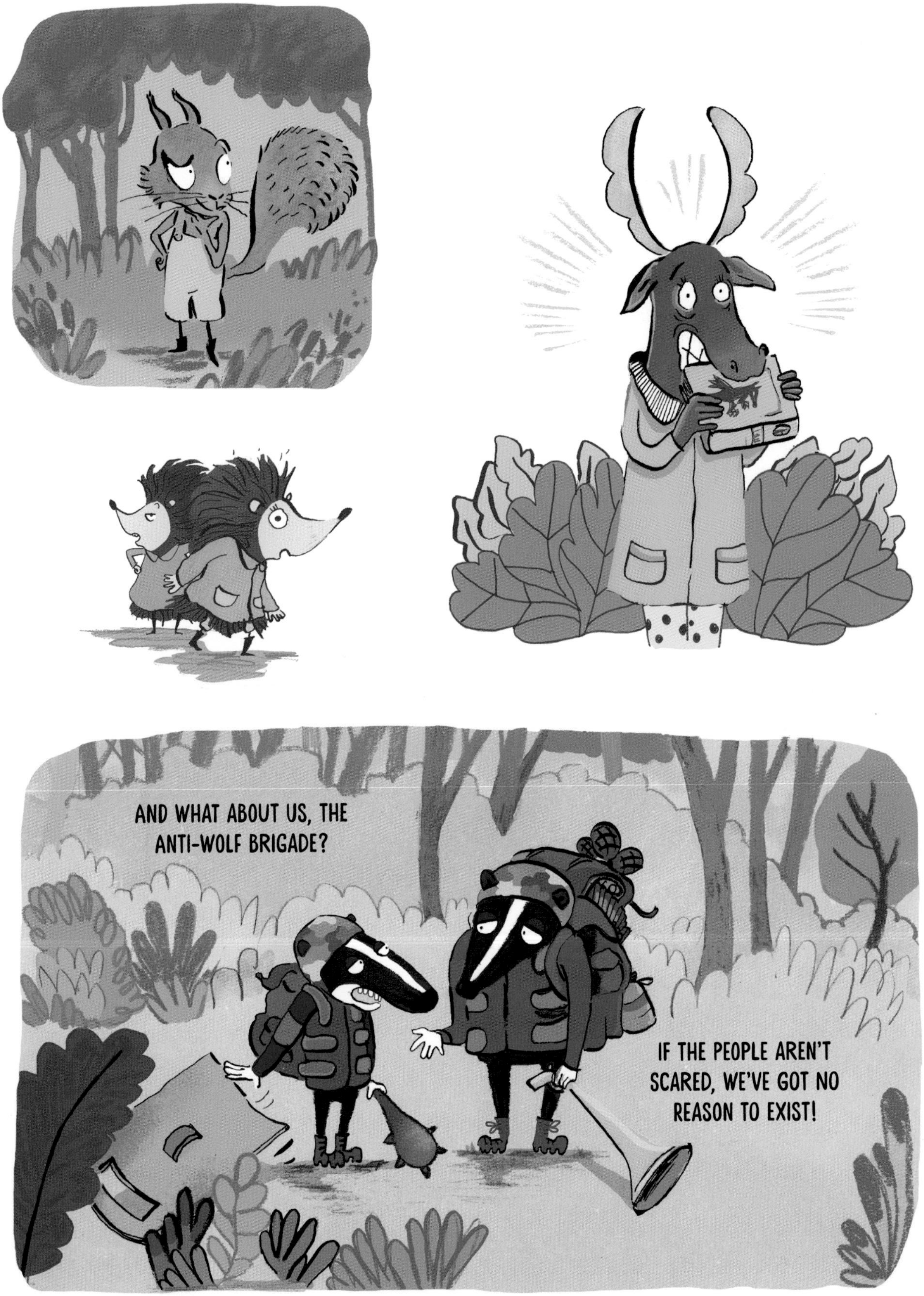
AND WHAT ABOUT US, THE ANTI-WOLF BRIGADE?
IF THE PEOPLE AREN'T SCARED, WE'VE GOT NO REASON TO EXIST!

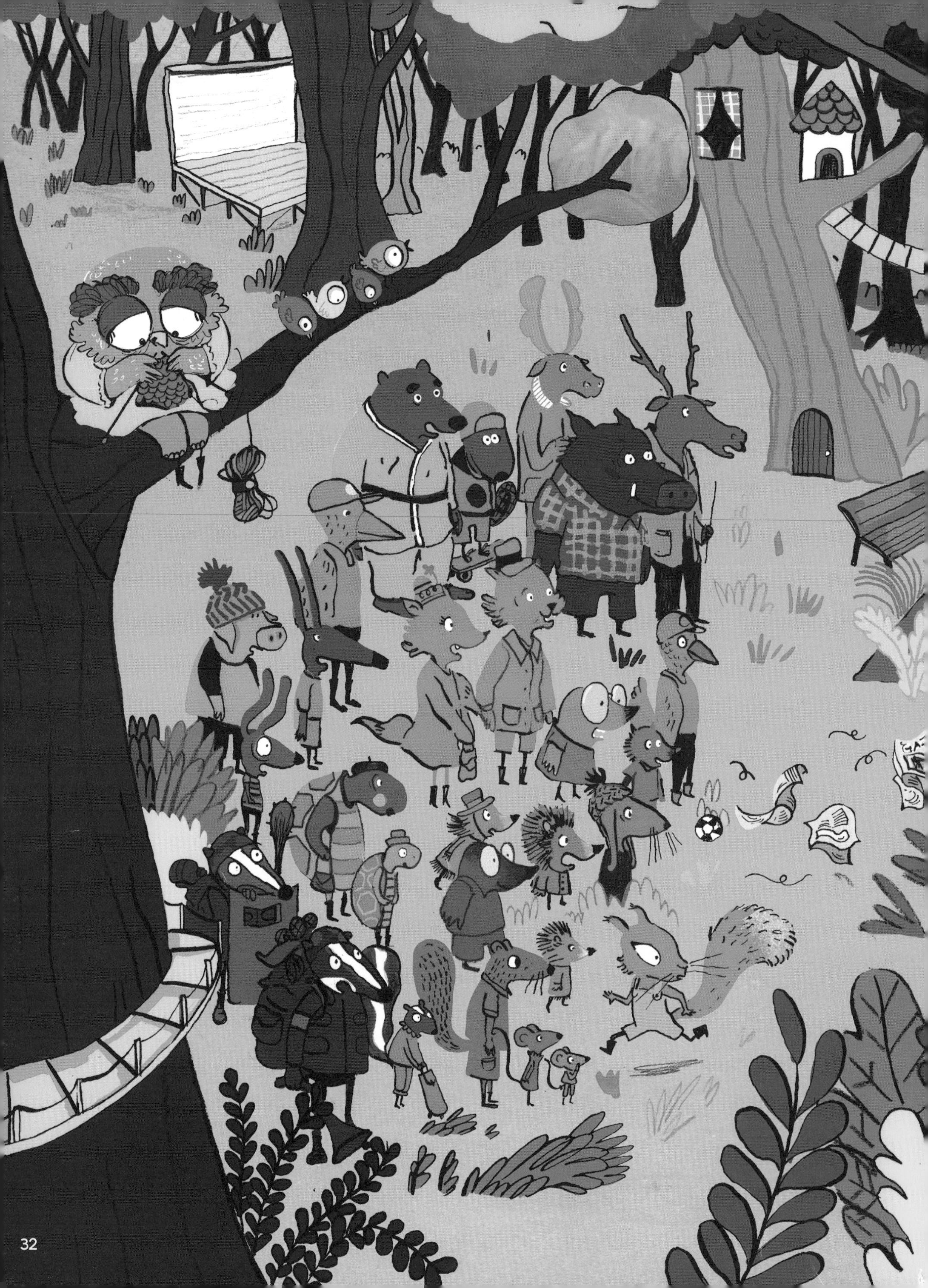

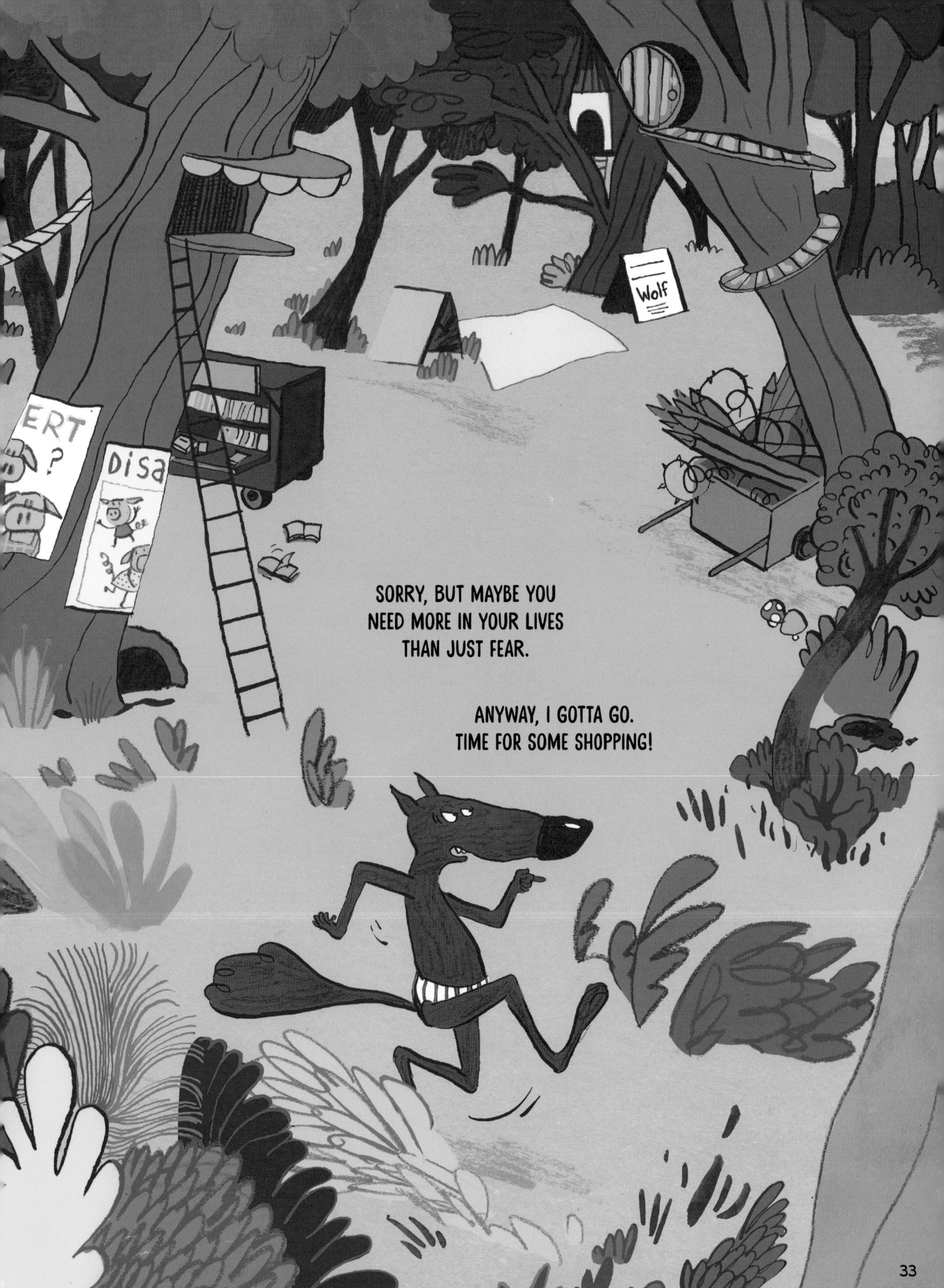
Wolf
SORRY, BUT MAYBE YOU NEED MORE IN YOUR LIVES THAN JUST FEAR.
ANYWAY, I GOTTA GO. TIME FOR SOME SHOPPING!

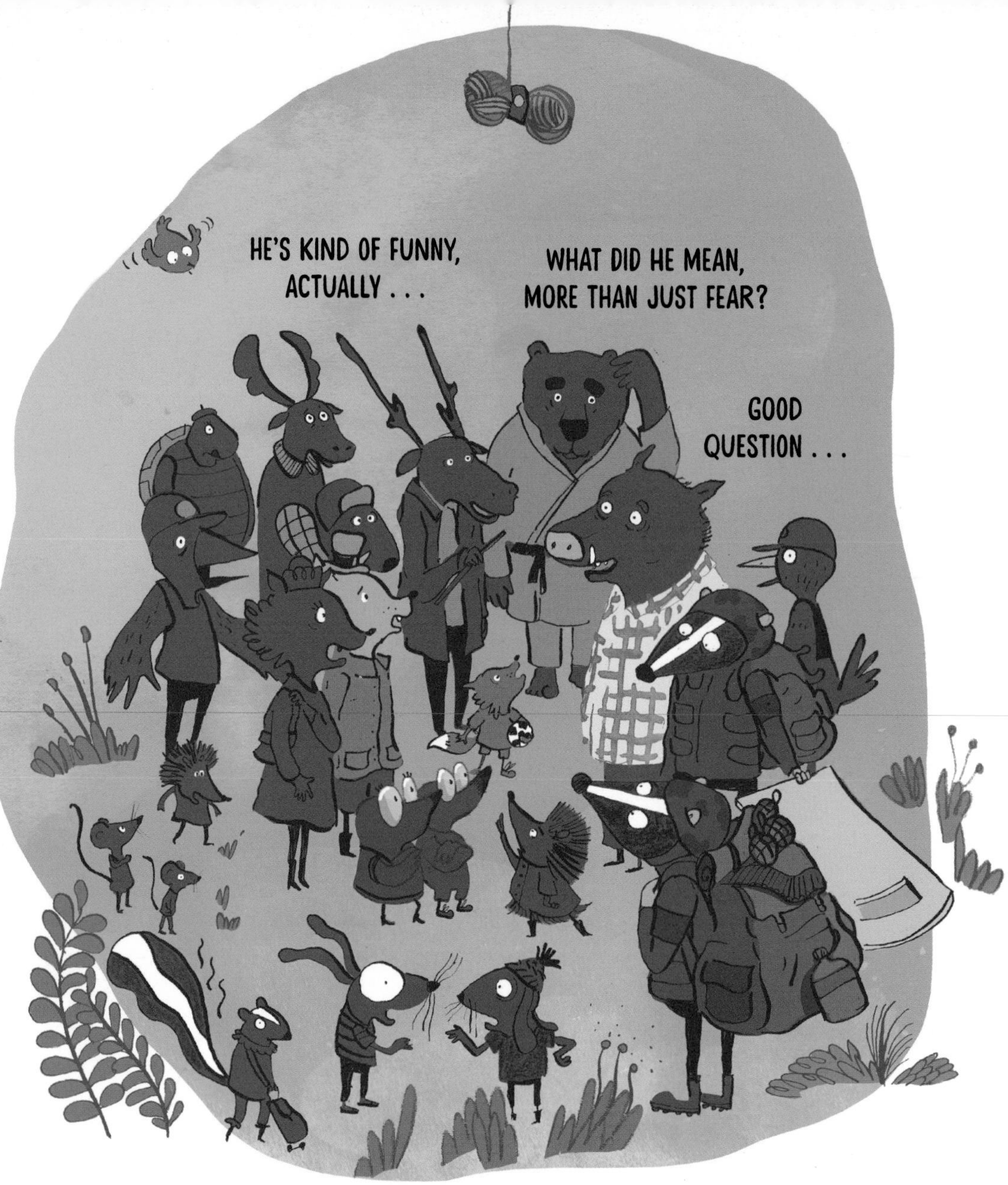
HE'S KIND OF FUNNY, ACTUALLY . . .
WHAT DID HE MEAN, MORE THAN JUST FEAR?
GOOD QUESTION . . .

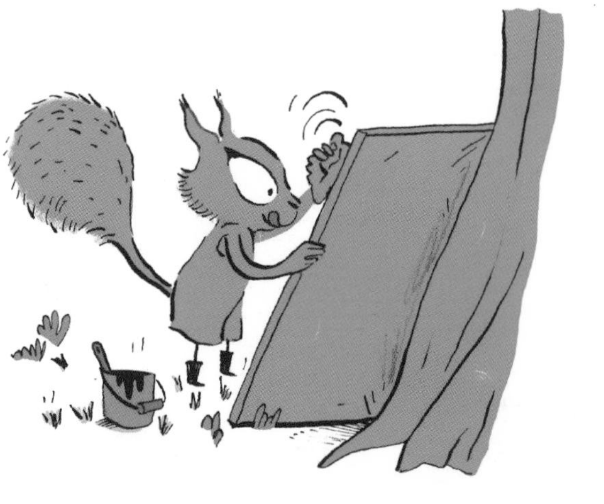

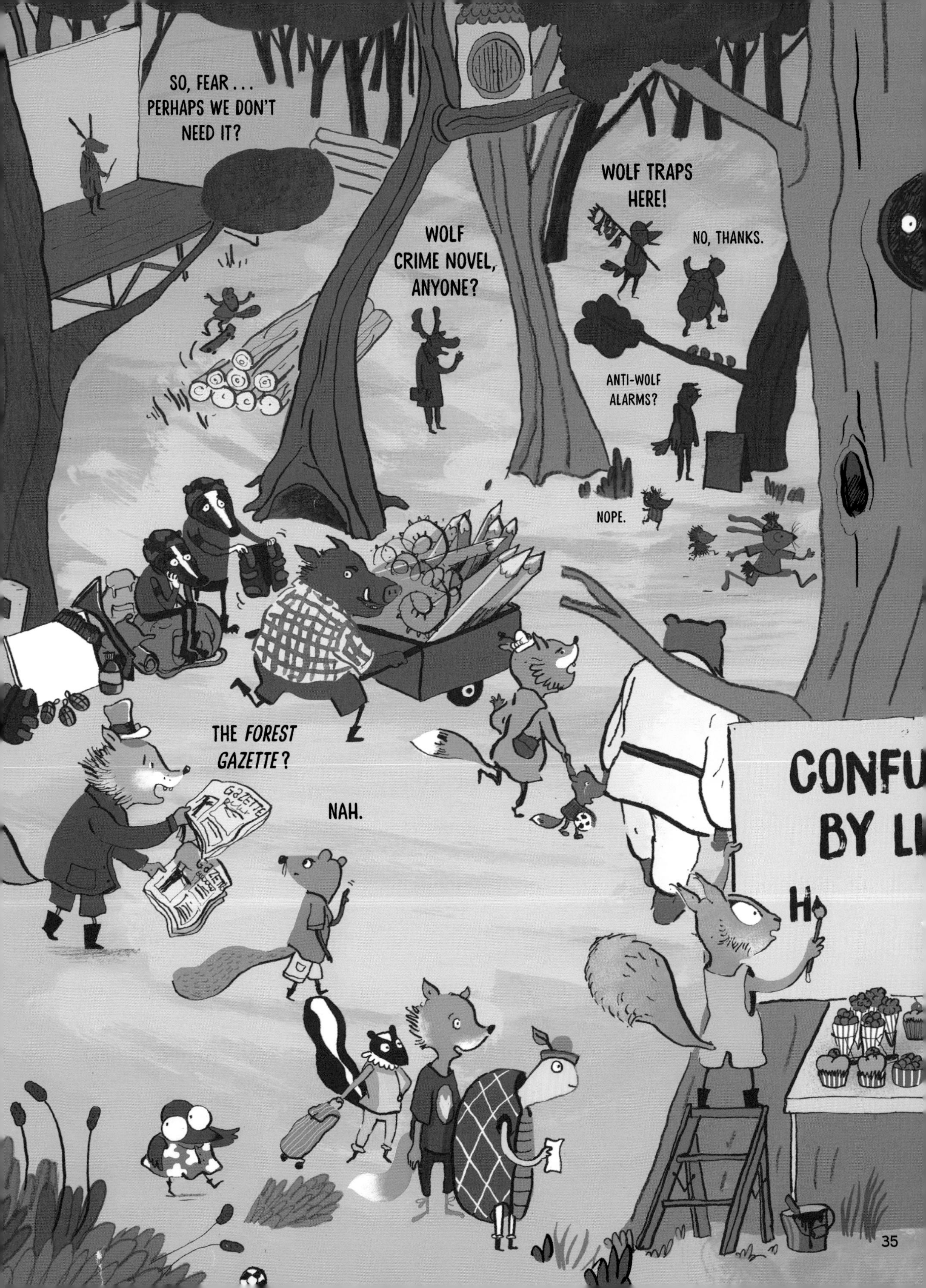

SO, FEAR . . .
PERHAPS WE DON'T
NEED IT?
WOLF
CRIME NOVEL,
ANYONE?
WOLF TRAPS
HERE!
NO, THANKS.
ANTI-WOLF
ALARMS?
NOPE.
THE *FOREST*
GAZETTE?
NAH.
CONFU
BY LI
H

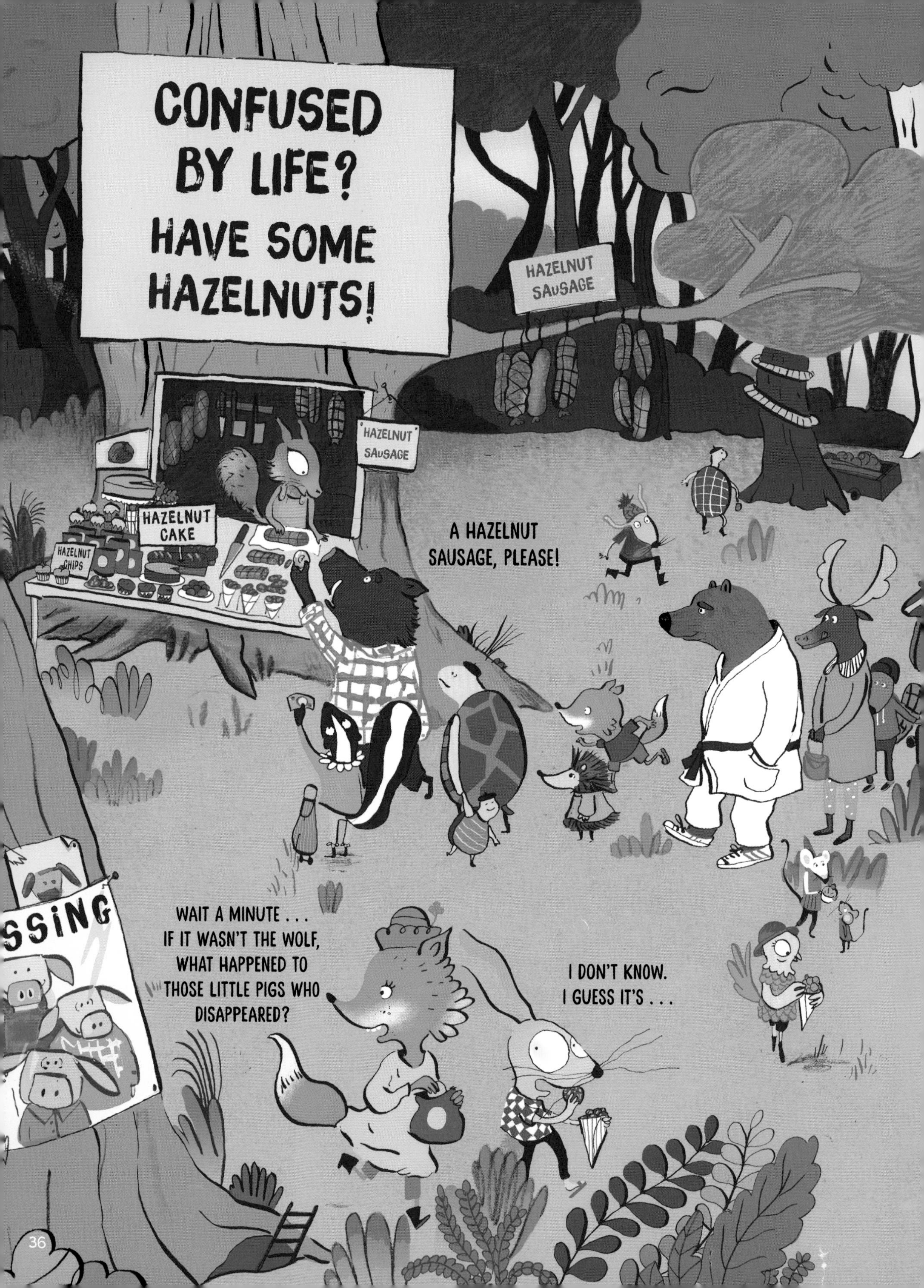
CONFUSED BY LIFE? HAVE SOME HAZELNUTS!
HAZELNUT SAUSAGE
HAZELNUT SAUSAGE
HAZELNUT CAKE
HAZELNUT CHIPS
A HAZELNUT SAUSAGE, PLEASE!
SSING
WAIT A MINUTE . . . IF IT WASN'T THE WOLF, WHAT HAPPENED TO THOSE LITTLE PIGS WHO DISAPPEARED?
I DON'T KNOW. I GUESS IT'S . . .

. . . A MYSTERY.

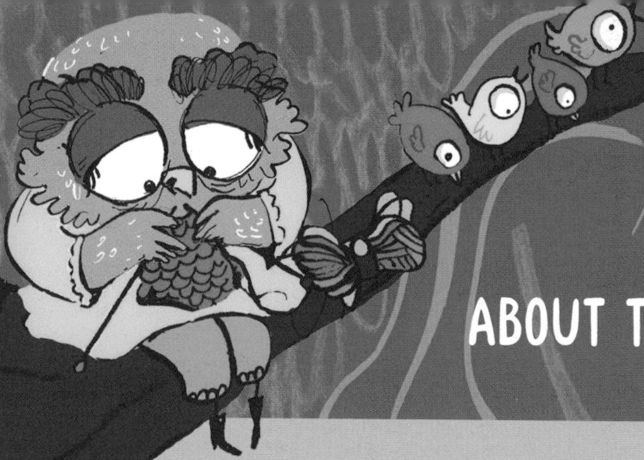

ABOUT THE CREATORS

Wilfrid Lupano

Wilfrid Lupano was born in Nantes, in the west of France, and spent most of his childhood in the southwestern city of Pau, France. He spent his childhood reading through his parents' comic book collection and enjoying role-playing games. He studied literature and philosophy, receiving a degree in English, before he began to script comics. He has written numerous graphic novels for French readers, including the series *Les Vieux Fourneaux* (in English, *The Old Geezers*). With this series, Lupano and Paul Cauuet first developed the idea that would become *The Wolf in Underpants*. Lupano once again lives in Pau after spending several years in the city of Toulouse.

Mayana Itoïz

Mayana Itoïz was born in the city of Bayonne, in the southwest of France, and studied at the *institut supérieur des arts de Toulouse* (School of Fine Arts in Toulouse), where she worked in many different mediums. In addition to being an illustrator and a cartoonist, she has taught art to high school students. She lives in the Pyrenees, near France's mountainous southern border, and splits her time between art, family, and travel.

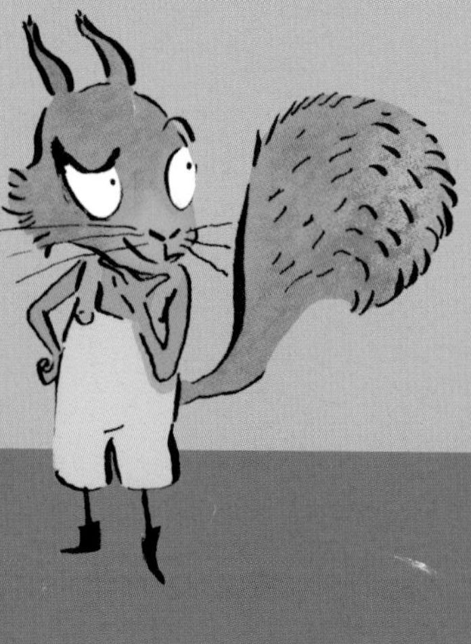

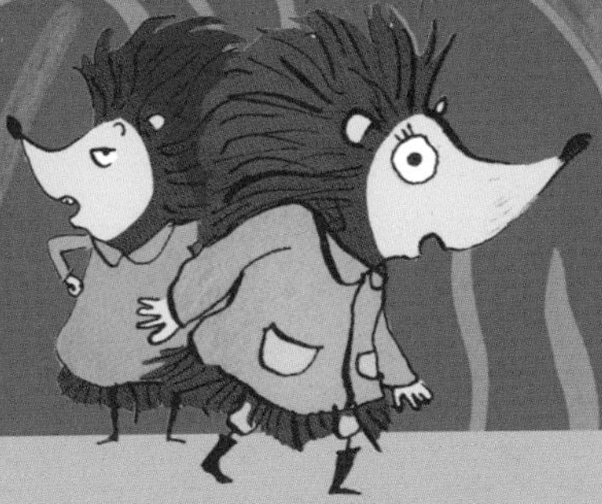

Paul Cauuet

Paul Cauuet was born in Toulouse and grew up in a family that encouraged his passion for drawing. He was also a fond reader of classic Franco-Belgian comics such as *Tintin* and *Asterix*. He studied at the University of Toulouse and went on to a career as a cartoonist. Cauuet and Wilfrid Lupano first collaborated on an outer-space comedy series before working together on *Les Vieux Fourneaux* (*The Old Geezers*).

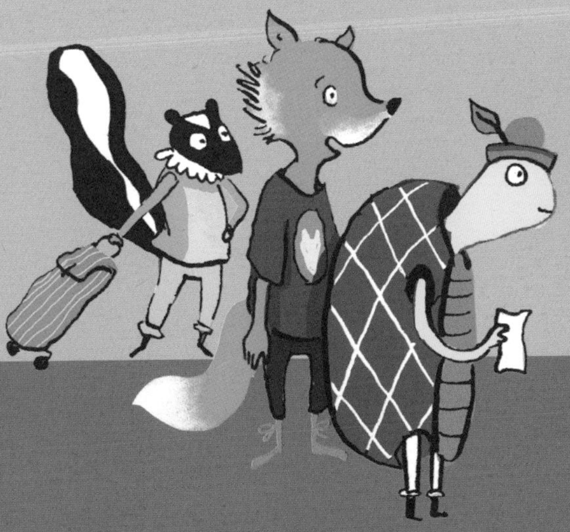

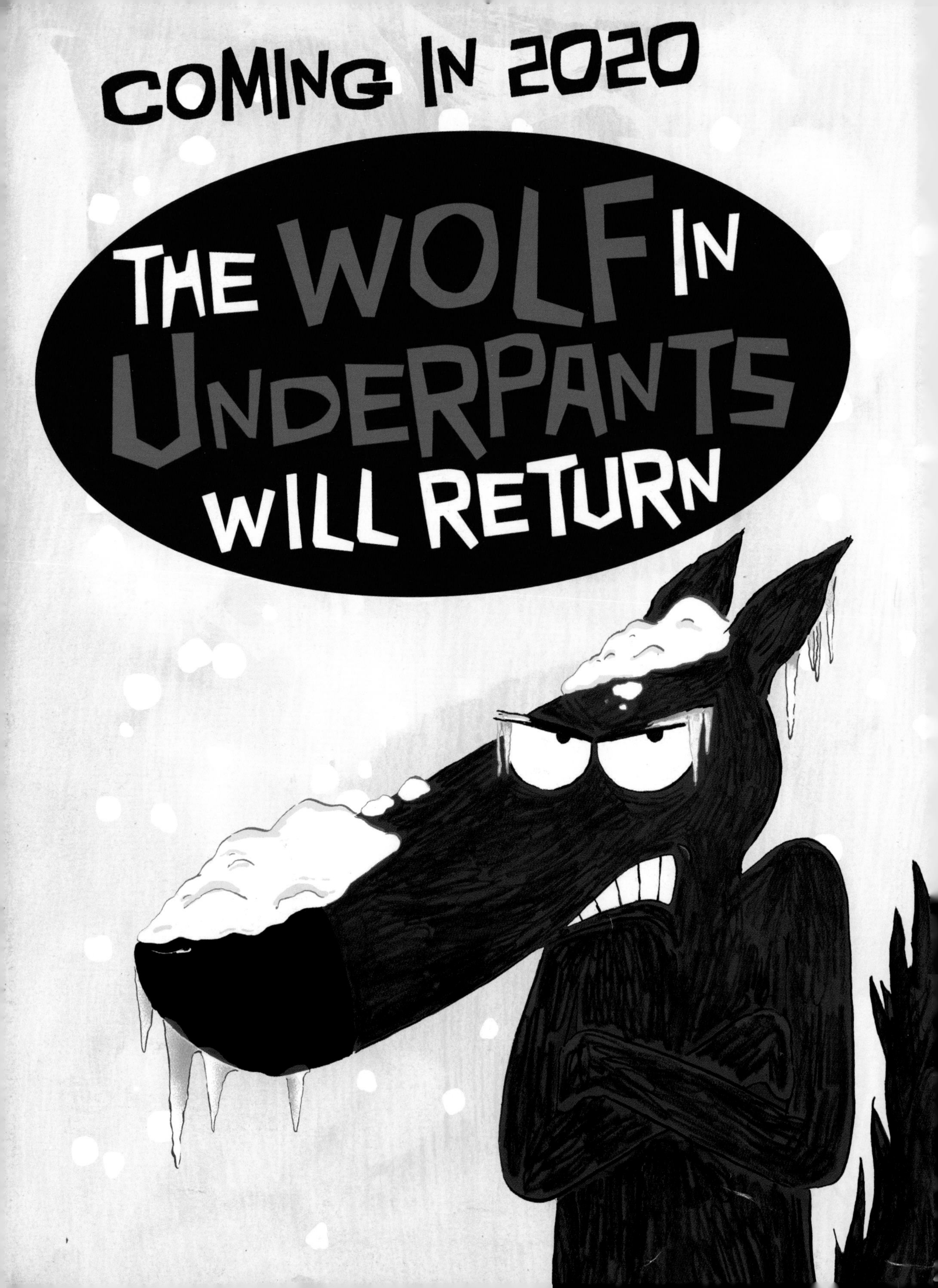
COMING IN 2020
THE WOLF IN UNDERPANTS WILL RETURN

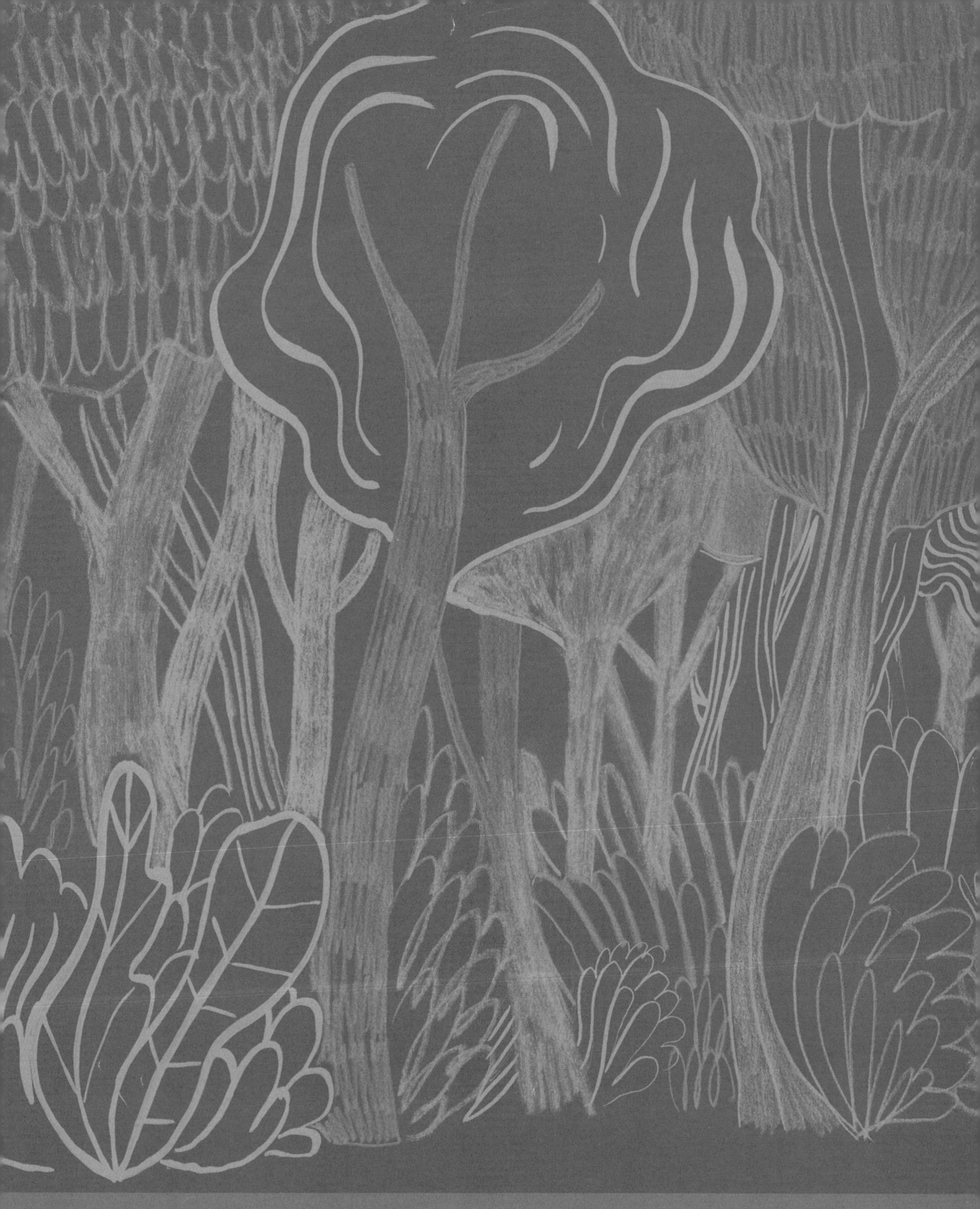

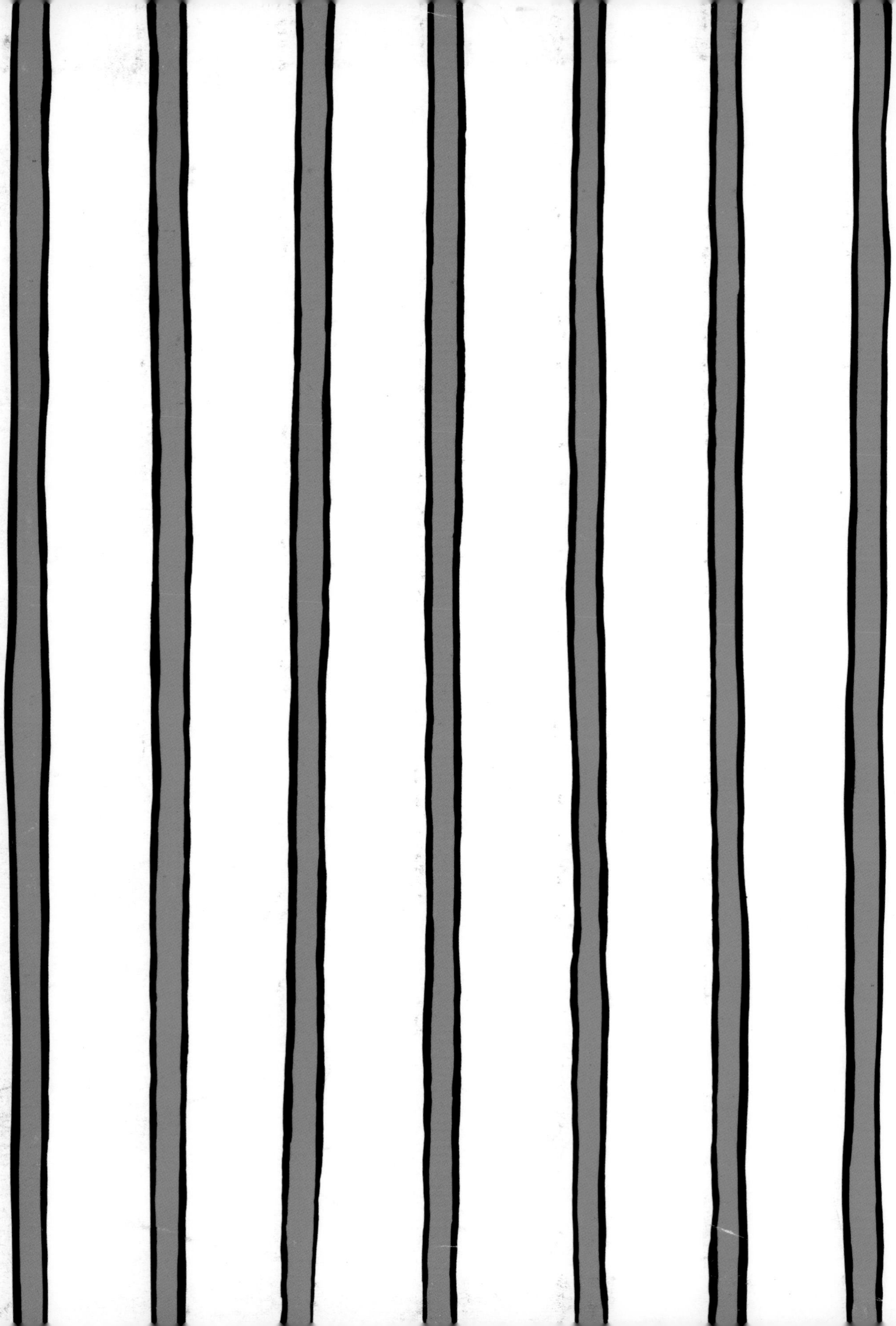